Covert Citadel

Alien Invasion Outback Australia

Rodney Jensen

Rodney Jensen Books

CiPcatalogue record for this book is available from the National Library of Australia.

Additional License Note

First published in Australia in 2022

Rodney Jensen Books
http://www.rodneyjensenbooks.com/

PO Box 443 Cammeray NSW 2062 Australia

ISBN 978-0-994-1668-3-8

CiPcatalogue record for this book is available from the National Library of Australia.

Dedication

This novel is dedicated to the memory of my mother, Elfrida Jensen, 1915-2001, co-author with Rolf Arthur Jensen of 'Colonial Architecture in South Australia', published by Rigby in 1980.

Elfrida taught me to read when I was an infant and her lively and creative mind infected me with a keen interest in the arts and sciences including an abiding love of SCI-FI as a teenager.

« »

About this book

'**Covert Citadel**' is the second volume of Rodney Jensen's **Covert Trilogy**, the first of which, '**Covert Messages**' was published in 2021 and is available on the main international book distribution sites including Amazon, Booktopia, Book Depository, Apple and others.

This story starts in 2042, an era when the effects of a serious pandemic across Australia have devastated the economy particularly for country dwellers. Sam Mitchell in her former life worked as an agent for a US-based agency, UFODD (an acronym for Unidentified Flying Object Defence Directorate), with her fellow agent Byron Lowe.

Now we reconnect with Sam and Byron, who have moved to a small sheep farm in Western New South Wales, in a remote part of the Australian Outback.

Rodney Jensen

Rodney Jensen

Review of Covert Citadel

"Much thought, imagination and care has gone into this chilling and provocative novel. It is a post-pandemic dystopian vision set in the out-back wastes of New South Wales and its devastated towns where a courageous few eke out a sparse existence. A young woman, Sam Mitchell provides hope, rallying a brave band of technologically adept survivors who stand up to the threat of a sinister and destructive alien power."

Jenny Towndrow.

PART 1
Pulling the Dragon's Tail
- 2042

Rodney Jensen

CHAPTER 1

The room's illumination dimmed and a holographic display appeared in the middle of the conference table. It showed a track in the bush, characteristic of the arid, semi-desert country of Central Australia.

The camera focussed on a man wearing dirty overalls. He wore a black necklace with a small electronic device shaped like a black pebble. It had a green and a yellow spot of light. The yellow was flashing at one second intervals. He sounded incoherent and desperate, as he gasped out a jumble of words.

"See that light," he said pointing at the device. "Yellow! Means no time left! Hurry. Don't touch me. You'll die. Seen it happen. Stay clear. Thank God you here. Must warn you bout Alien City."

"Alien City?" the voice behind the camera sounded bemused, humouring.

"Living hell mate, living hell. You got to stop 'em, shut it down. Bots running the place, advanced AI's. They're using us—hybrids like. No built in human protection there. Couldn't give the slightest shit about us. Any excuse you're gone. Herding others into the production lines to make up for the killings. Working us to death, non-stop building. Shipping stuff for other places like Alien City ..."

"Where is this Alien City?" Camera voice interrupted.

"Good distance from here," he twisted his head back down the track to indicate direction. "Been walking forever! Losing track—I think got out three nights ago. Not much time left. In the mountains somewhere, but most's underground. Got to stop 'em, they got plans. I don't …" The man stopped in mid-sentence his knees buckled and he collapsed.

Momentarily the picture went haywire as whoever was holding the camera sprang into action before the screen went blank.

CHAPTER 2

The hot afternoon sun, high in the western sky, was beating down through a dusty haze onto the brown acres of a small country property. For many people the combination of accelerating climate change and recurring pandemics over the past two decades had forced them into a subsistence living outside the cities.

Beneath the corrugated iron roof of a dilapidated shearing shed, a slight female figure in an open necked check shirt and broad brimmed hat was on her knees, flailing at an incessant swarm of flies and wiping the sweat off her forehead while trying to adjust the controls of a shearing bot. An anxious ram covered in a thick woollen coat was looking on, stamping his front hoof impatiently as he waited to be shorn.

Sam Mitchell was no classical beauty with her short cut blonde hair, snub nose and distinctive gap between her front two teeth. But her bright blue eyes with surrounding crinkle marks and full mouth presented a pleasing homely look, except on this morning when a shadow of impatience was marring her features. With her forehead scrunched in a frown of concentration, her lips pursed, she fiddled with the settings on the display screen, feeling the radiant heat on her back, finally banging her fist on the casing in exasperation when it stubbornly refused to do what she wanted of it. Her frown grew deeper as a sudden alert from the holo in the back pocket of her jeans distracted her attention. She tried ignoring the call, but it grew ever more insistent, continuing for a full minute before she finally relented and pulled it out.

Rodney Jensen

"Yes—it's not a good time I'm afraid," she said without bothering to look more closely at the caller's ID.

"I need to speak to you now, it's urgent."

The sound of Byron's voice caught her unprepared. He'd been taking part in an outback bush-bash with some mates and left strict instructions not to be contacted except for emergencies.

"I wasn't expecting you. Is everything all right?"

"No everything's not all right. We need to meet up in the next 12 hours."

Sam was feeling more and more perplexed. "Where did you have in mind? I thought you were having some fun with your mates somewhere remote."

"It is quite remote, but I haven't been completely straight with you about what I've been doing. There are good reasons and I promise I'll explain as soon as we meet. I've just loaded coordinates of where you need to meet me into the MAG's Pilot. It's a few hours driving, but it'll know how to get there now."

"This is not a good time Byron. I'm in the middle of shearing. Is this all you can tell me? Why all the cloak and dagger?"

"I promise you it's safer you stay in the dark for the moment. You'll see why as soon as we meet."

"Okay—I can't just drop everything. What do I do with the sheep? I need to pack a few things, and come to think of it, what do I need to bring?"

"Don't worry about that. Just bring some water and make sure the emergency spares are where they should be. We've got everything here. Let the sheep into the dam paddock. There's enough pasture to keep them going for a while. I don't want you

alerting anyone to our movements. Leave after dark if possible. Just lock everything up before you leave and come when you can. I can't at this stage say when or whether we'll be back."

"Shit this must be serious. Are you OK? Are you sure there's nothing else I can do here, or bring?"

"No, everything's been covered. We just need to have you here?"

"Who's we?"

"Please Sam you'll have to trust me on this and I have to go. All will be explained, I promise. I'll see you tomorrow morning."

Sam stared at her now blank holo screen. She pressed the return key, but immediately saw a **CODE UNAVAILABLE** message.

"Well, fuck you!" she fumed aloud at the mystified ram, the only available male she could take it out on. Turning her attention back towards the bot, she hit the cancel key and switched the unit off, pushing it back into its holding bay with a slam that shook the whole enclosure. She opened the gate to the holding pen and shooed the ram back into the paddock. Then she ejected the sheared ones in the same direction, not caring that the flock would be mixed up. *What does it matter anyway?*

CHAPTER 3

S am surfaced from her disturbed night looking dishevelled and bleary-eyed. Lifting her head a fraction she groaned as the interior of the maglev all-terrain vehicle (commonly known as 'MAG') came into focus, the seats piled with the clutter that she'd hastily thrown aboard before setting off.

Then her expression changed from un-focused to full alert, something was amiss. After an interminable night in the tossing MAG, avoiding ruts, potholes, even the odd ants' nest, it had been difficult to settle. Countering the nauseous sensation of a hovercraft in a heavy swell, she'd finally drifted off, leaving FRED in charge (her name for the on-board navigation and driving system) an essential piece of software she loved to hate.

It must have been the silence and stillness that had woken her up. *Why has the MAG stopped?*

She fumbled around for the GX-Laser hand weapon she'd put in the glove box, taking no chances. There'd been too many reports of vigilantes roaming areas as remote as this in search of supplies, sex and slave labour in the wake of the pandemic.

The pandemic had been the game changer to throw the globe into anarchy and send government control into retreat. The uncontrolled spread of the deadly bio-agent had decimated the world's population nearly 10 years before, and its shock waves would continue to be felt for many years to come. Australia was left with a population of less than 10 million and they were mostly concentrated in the main capital cities, leaving the bush a largely depleted and lawless territory. For Sam, a safe and stable world was already a distant memory and this was no time to forget her own security.

The windscreen was covered in dew, the cabin feeling like a freezer. She fumbled around to find and un-fasten her seatbelt, scrambled outside, and recoiled at an even more icy wall of dawn air. The first orange beams of the sun were creating a surrealist desert-scape with clouds of smoky vapour drifting across the unbroken sea of orange tinged, silver grey scrub. Within this beautiful panorama, the MAG's odd alienness seemed a strange intrusion in an otherwise unblemished natural wilderness.

After a short break she returned to the comparative warmth of her driver's seat. She started punching buttons, frowning at the lack of any clue as to what was causing the seemingly unscheduled layover. The energy store was showing a healthy 60% level. A green animated arrow confirmed that the rising sun was already starting to charge the battery. She checked the travel log and it was reading the start time as 20:45 the night before and finishing at 05:15. Her watch was showing 05:55.

"Is this our destination—there's nothing here?" She addressed her question to the Console.

A synthetic voice responded from a tinny sounding speaker: "Your journey is complete. Please refer to trip log. Do you require any further information?"

She paused for a second before snapping back: "Display a ground map of this location!"

"Information classified," the computer responded. "Do you require an alternative such as large scale map with exclusion zone identified?"

"Of course!" Her patience had evaporated with the morning mist.

A featureless map came on the screen showing virtually nothing except the road leaving their origin point to the east of Bourke, proceeding almost due west and then entering a blank section with nothing marked but a small icon somewhere near its middle.

Sam touched the icon with her fingertip. "Is this our MAG?"

"That is correct."

"How far are we from our origin point?"

"Four hundred and thirty seven point six five kilometres."

"Do you have any further programmed instructions?"

"No—all previous advice given is as shown. The trip is completed. Those were my only instructions, except that once we have reached this point, further travel is forbidden."

"I don't believe this. Do you mean that you are unable to take me home?"

"Unless you have administrative override privileges, I regret that is not possible."

The only thing preventing Sam from taking an axe to Fred was the frustrating realisation that he might well still be her only chance of survival. "Can you send Byron a message informing him of our arrival at this place?"

"That has already been sent."

"Was there any acknowledgement?"

"Yes"

"This is like getting blood out of a stone! What did it say for God's sake?"

"*Await further instructions*, that is all."

A wave of angry relief washed through her. *I must be patient—at least Byron knows I'm here.* After an hour, she took another turn outside the MAG, staying close in case there were any new communications coming in. She eased herself out of the cabin and stretched her legs, breathing in the fresh desert air. She could feel her anxiety melt away, replaced by a sense of enjoyment at the overwhelming peace and freedom in this vast and remote arena.

At last, the briefest spark of light in the distance to the right of the track caught her attention. As she focused more carefully, she could see a faint line of dust following a rapidly moving dot. It gradually resolved into the shape of another MAG, its windscreen sending the occasional sun-reflected flash her way. It was still too far off to guess who owned it.

She reacted quickly, clambered aboard the MAG, locking the door after her. She watched calmly, fearing the worst. What she could now recognise as an unmarked military style vehicle, had turned into her slightly wider track and parked alongside her. A man emerged, wearing full protective gear, and paused to remove his helmet. He waved in her general direction.

She sprang out of her MAG boiling with frustration and relief at seeing Byron's face.

Rodney Jensen

"Don't tell me this is something to do with UFODD?" Byron was in uniform, similar to one Sam owned but had stored away years before. It was the same distinctive design and colour, and bore an unusual logo on the breast pocket, a simple motif displaying the acronym *'UFODD'* for **U**nidentified **F**lying **O**bject **D**efense **D**irectorate.

"I'm really sorry Honey. This whole operation's highly classified. I've only been allowed to bring you to the edge of the exclusion zone unescorted. I'm sorry I wasn't waiting for you here when you arrived, but there have been new developments, even since last night."

The uniform confirmed her suspicions. It was the giveaway for all the secrecy. She had mixed feelings about UFODD. She at least owed the organisation something for facilitating her meeting and eventually marrying Byron, but it also brought back some memories she preferred kept sealed in the past.

Byron gave his wife a hug, but she found it difficult to return his warmth given what he had put her through without explanation. "I was really worried about you. What on Earth's going on? What exclusion zone?"

"Having worked for UFODD in the past when we were experiencing the most serious post-Covid 19 global pandemic, it shouldn't surprise you that they're still paranoid about contamination from outside. This procedure's just to make absolutely certain that we don't bring anything back into the Base. You'll hear about the rest very soon. It's best you get the story from the boss first. Now you need to put this on," Byron handed Sam her own set of protective gear in a duffle bag. "You can leave the helmet off for the time, but once we get to the main entrance you'll have to put it on."

Sam ripped off her outer clothes and threw them into the back of the MAG before donning her protective gear without saying anything further.

"We'll need to head for the base in convoy. We can't leave our MAG here. Just follow me as soon as you're ready."

They drove in tandem along the narrow track for three kilometres before reaching a razor wire fence stretching to the horizon in both directions. A heavy duty swing gate, wide enough to admit the largest MAGs, barred any further progress until Byron had placed his face close to the retinal scanning window as instructed. The lock responded with a green light and a pre-recorded synthetic voice warning that they were under constant surveillance and had only 60 seconds to enter before the gate would re-lock.

As they began their drive via a long and straight dirt-road Sam was mulling over what had taken place seven years earlier, when she had worked with Byron in UFODD on a strange case involving alien contact. A man known as 'Sens', his girlfriend Meg and his dog had attended the opening of a new Aboriginal housing settlement, the 'Muldoon Estate', honouring a highly respected local Aboriginal Elder. They became implicated in the mysterious abduction of Senator John Williams, who was the head of the Australian Graziers Party. He was well regarded in the region but had earned a reputation for various property deals that had lined his pocket. Williams was in the middle of his oration, when the abduction took place.

According to reports, Sen's dog had led a pack of other dogs in a ring around the Senator as he was making his address. Many of the onlookers had observed an 'alien looking wedge shaped craft' appearing in the sky above the audience, and everyone surrounding the presentation became enveloped in impenetrable mist. The dogs began howling in chorus as the mist was briefly illuminated by a powerful cone of light. The dogs stopped howling abruptly and the mist cleared to reveal that the Senator had vanished.

In what came to be known as the 'Muldoon Incident', the strange behaviour of the dogs, and in particular, the one who belonged to Sens, was never explained.

Sam and Byron had interrogated Sens and Meg but learned little. Captain Sens, revealed he was a retired QANTAS pilot, and claimed his dog was channelling messages from an alien intelligence nest, who preferred to communicate with him via his dog. The powers that be were sceptical about this claim but no alternative explanation was ever identified. Sam and Byron were not invited to renew their contracts one year later but by this time they had fallen for each other, despite being polar opposites in many ways, and were content to take up farming and leave the matter of alien incursion to others.

Bloody UFODD again—why did he lie to me about all this?—he could have discussed it instead of going behind my back—to hell with their security protocols, he should have ignored them—I definitely did have a need to know—he should have realised that—arrogant bastard—trips with his mates huh!

There was no ready answer she could think of to this question as they continued their drive along another six kilometres of track, finally arriving at what looked like the entrance portal to an underground facility. The portal was impossible to see until they were almost on top of it. They progressed down a steep driveway into a tunnel. The end was hidden in darkness but ceiling lights began switching on, leading them to another gateway and sentry box.

Security requested Byron show his ID before the gate slowly slid open and allowed the two MAGs to enter. They found themselves in a parking area with no more than a dozen vehicles already occupying bays and spare capacity for many others. They parked, and walked across to the only exit point marked by a lift. The lift door opened and shut soundlessly behind them, beginning what seemed like an interminable descent. The lift interior was devoid of any features and it was impossible to tell how far down they were going, but it seemed like a very deep hole. For Sam the prospect of returning to UFODD in such strange circumstances made her want to turn right around now and never come back.

CHAPTER 4

The lift finally came to rest and the doors slid open to reveal two uniformed personnel, also wearing protective clothing and masks. They guided Sam and Byron through a series of decontamination and bio-testing procedures to minimise the risk of bringing the disease into the installation, before the two emerged, freshly showered and suited. They were taken through an airlock and escorted down a long corridor and shown into a conference room where three people were seated around a boardroom table deep in conversation.

A mature serious looking woman, who seemed to be in charge, introduced herself to Sam. "Good morning I'm Dr Lesley Harcourt," she said.

"What happened to Graves. He was the head of UFODD Asia Pacific when I was on staff?"

The question seemed to unbalance Harcourt. "I believe Graves returned to the United States to be closer to his daughter. She was attending university there, I think," Harcourt said finally. "I had forgotten you knew him. He was in UFODD before my time. I believe that he was given early retirement following what is now referred to in our files as the 'Muldoon Incident'. You were involved in investigating it too, were you not?"

Sam nodded, not wanting to be distracted from hearing more about Graves. In the awkward silence that followed, she finally tried to get at the truth again. "He wasn't that old to be put out to pasture was he?"

"As you know there was a lot going on at the time Graves was in charge here with the pandemic and the 'Muldoon Incident'. From what I've read on file, it seems the powers that be felt that he could have handled things better," Harcourt stated flatly. "Please do sit down. You've arrived at an appropriate moment to join us in our discussion."

"I'm completely in the dark about what's going on here. But let me guess—something to do with another alien incursion? Perhaps you'd care to enlighten me, why have I've been called here?"

"I can understand why you're feeling angry Sam, but Byron has only been doing things the way I asked him, I can assure you," Harcourt informed her quietly.

"Yes, he's made that clear. Why the need for such security. It must be serious!"

"It is—very serious. As you may recall at the time of the 'Muldoon Incident', our intelligence uncovered ample evidence to suggest extra-terrestrials were responsible. Higher governmental authorities tried to play that down with the alternative theory that the incident was a hoax. But having read the files it clearly wasn't a hoax, at least in my assessment. Further evidence for the extra-terrestrial theory was the mysterious disappearance of the two main players involved—Sens and Meg, immediately following the incident. There was also Sens' dog, 'Marshall', a vital and virtually overlooked player at the time, although we finally tracked them down."

Sam nodded, waiting for Harcourt to get to the point. "Muldoon remains a mystery to this day and who knows—maybe the Aliens did have something to do with the disappearance of the Senator. As you know beside Muldoon, there was strong evidence that alien forces had abducted other animals in South East Queensland, native dingoes in one instance and fruit bats in another," said Harcourt. "Anyway that's all past history and we never really got to verify Sens and Meg's story."

Sam, suddenly hit her forehead, guessing where the conversation was heading.

"Don't tell me! The aliens are back aren't they?" she said.

"And that is why you are here, Sam. But let me first tell you more about this facility. It is probably no coincidence that it was set up shortly after the 'Muldoon Incident'."

"Again I'm guessing," said Sam. "But maybe it was because the old UFODD base was far too near to Bourke and posed a security threat to the whole of that region."

"You're close, but the reasons were more political than that. Too many people were in the know about both the 'Muldoon Incident'. There was an association in many peoples' minds between those events and the pandemic. The presence of the base also became public knowledge and it was thought to be only a matter of time that its security would be breached, making continuing operations untenable."

"That's probably why Byron and I were shown the door. Except that it appears to have been me who was shown the door and Byron retained—behind my back!"

Harcourt continued, as though she had not noticed Sam's resentment. "The other factor was that the original Bourke base was not optimally designed to withstand a biological agent as virulent as 'HRNX-0', the one that caused the pandemic. To cut a long story short, this installation was set up to address both of these needs, namely to be a safe facility against any bio-agent and also a communications base for future alien contact. It is the latter function which is already proving its worth."

Sam turned angrily to face Byron. "And you've known about this all along! All that garbage about bush-bashing weekends! Why is it that I've been kept out of the loop?"

Harcourt jumped in before Byron had a chance to respond. "UFODD were putting new policies into place after Muldoon, and one thing they were strongly against were partner situations of any type, particularly husband and wife teams," she said, sounding increasingly defensive. "Close relationships of any sort were frowned on, because of the high risk of compromising one another's security, particularly if either of them were to fall into enemy hands. So we had to make a choice, and given the probability that you might want to start raising a family at some point ..."

"Unbelievable and presumptuous!" interjected Sam. "If I'd heard such an excuse one hundred years ago I'd have been disgusted. Much as I respect Byron's professionalism, did my actual merit ever come into play?"

"I can't go there," replied Harcourt smoothly, "since I had nothing to do with the decision. But I have to acknowledge that the security threat is certainly a valid issue and there is also a 'need to know' aspect involved in what is highly classified information."

"So what's changed now?" asked Sam, cutting to the chase.

"In this case there's relevant history which involves both of you. Furthermore, something specific has come up. Since you two are the closest to having any direct knowledge of the Nest's existence, we would like you to lead our inquiries as a team from now on. It will be necessary Sam, for you to confirm your existing security clearances and confidentiality regulations, we are still holding them on file. That is of course if you're willing to assist?"

There was a pregnant and embarrassing pause as Sam thought how she should formulate a suitably withering response.

Harcourt finally broke the silence, clearing her throat before continuing in a more subdued voice. "Believe me I can understand your feelings. As I've said, I really had no say into which of you should originally be inducted into their new role." She paused for a moment to reflect. Sam could see that she clearly felt embarrassed to be defending the indefensible from her own point of view.

"I also want to tell you that I've had my share of blatantly partisan and unfair job decisions. No hear me out!" She held up her hand as Sam was about to interject again. "But the real reason for a change of heart is we find ourselves confronted by … something which maybe we should have anticipated earlier."

"What exactly is going on," asked Sam, her mounting interest rivalling her anger.

"There has been a sighting. A man was picked up claiming to have escaped from an alien base he called 'Alien City'. The man was delirious, and died before he could tell us much. But what he did say was of sufficient concern for us to want to investigate it further."

"And?"

"He spoke of people being captured and turned into bionic slaves. He was terrified of an alien force that was expanding to other sites and aliens who were clearly unconcerned about protecting human life. He was dead when we got him back here, and it definitely wasn't due to the pandemic. The device he was wearing around his neck we are convinced is alien technology. We could find no other way to remove it other than severing his head from his body during the autopsy. Our efforts to scan its workings have failed completely since it is able to screen out anything we throw at it."

"You're investigating this 'Alien City'?"

"Yes we think we have worked out the position from the man's very rough description. There is an area of mountains, the only mountains within three hundred kilometres of here, but we've yet to investigate it further."

"Why the delay?"

"Something else has cropped up," she said. "It's why we have asked you to come here."

"Oh of course—because the Nest's back as well!" said Sam again.

"Yes I'm afraid so. You really do have remarkable intuition," she acknowledged sourly. "Let me show you this communique I received the day before yesterday, not long after we made contact with the escaped victim. The message appeared without any warning on my holo." She handed Sam the device.

The message was curt:

"THE DIRECTOR UFODD ASIA PACIFIC

The Nest wish to restore communications with Earth. We are pleased to nominate a former member of your staff Special Agent Sam Mitchell. Our first link is scheduled for Noon on February 24 Central Australian time and may be held anywhere within your headquarters. Please expedite this request, no substitutions shall be accepted.

MESSAGE ENDS."

"Why me?" Sam said, finally breaking the silence.

"We don't know. We were as surprised as you," said Harcourt. "We are guessing it has to do with your previous connection with Sens and his dog, and this evidence of 'Alien City' is surely no coincidence."

"It is not the way they've communicated with us before."

"Yes that's true, and it opens up another possibility that may be of even greater concern to us," she said.

"Another extra-terrestrial force, you mean?"

"Exactly. Assuming that the Nest's approach towards us is benign, maybe Alien City represents another extreme, one which they equally want to combat."

"Sound like we're speculating on speculations!" said Byron who had been sitting quietly observing their exchange all this time.

"That maybe the case," said Harcourt, "but what choice do we have other than to listen to what they have to say. As things stand …" she paused to take a deep breath, "I believe we could be powerless to eradicate this Alien City. Our only hope is that the Nest will give us the means to do that. But as you can appreciate, the contact time they have set is less than a week off. There's much to do."

CHAPTER 5

There was a hush of expectancy in the observation room where Sam had been set up to await her contact with the Nest. She was seated at a plain table with nothing but her holo and a digital timer. The room had been prepared to record whatever happened in video. There were also sensors for a variety of other frequencies that could conceivably be used for communications.

Sam was nervously tapping a pen on the desk feeling on the one hand curious to know more and on the other hand fearing the power this alien network held, not only over her, but the entire world she knew.

She jolted in her seat as she heard a soft voice inside her head. It had the same sound and intonation she immediately recognised as "Leila" whom she had first communicated with some years earlier while assisting UFODD in its inquiries. The voice was authoritative yet gentle.

Hello Sam, please do not be alarmed. It is regrettable that we need to communicate once again, but the situation has progressed from when we last spoke.

"What developments are you talking about?" she asked aloud for the benefit of her observers.

We previously alluded to our concern that our opposing network which we call the "Aggressives" were breaching our long standing treaty by making incursions into this sector of the galaxy. They have now commenced what amounts to an invasion of your planet. If we make any overt move to counter their plans, it will inevitably escalate the situation. Instead we prefer to brief you on how to mount your own defences…

"I really think this should be shared with my colleagues. This is far too serious a matter for me to negotiate!"

> *As before we will not allow this discussion to be recorded and your organisation must rely on what we must explain to you alone. You may share what you can recall of this discussion but it is entirely up to you and your colleagues to decide how best to proceed.*

At this blunt and bulldozer-like response, Sam wanted to terminate the conversation immediately. It was only the realisation that as the stakes were so high, she had little option but to learn what else lay in store for her world and whether there was any hope that the Aggressives could be counteracted.

For the others, Sam's one sided conversation lasting for the best part of an hour was frustrating in the extreme. They could only guess at what she was hearing and would have to rely on her to fill in the gaps.

"It was the weirdest thing," Sam said at her initial de-briefing. "It was same contact I heard previously when I was working on the Muldoon Incident and other reports connected with Sens, his girlfriend and his dog."

"This situation is far from ideal. I don't like the way they are keeping us and everyone else but you in the dark," Harcourt remarked.

"Bottom line is that the Nest claim there is another alien force at work, whom they call the 'Aggressives'. It seems that they are responsible for this Alien City and if unchecked, they're set to annihilate the human race. The Nest can only advise us on how to defeat them."

Rodney Jensen

"Can we afford to ignore this warning, if it's to be believed, and an even bigger 'if', *are we definitely on the right side?*" Harcourt pondered.

Sam paused for a moment to make sure they had taken in what she'd been saying. "Anyway, give me some time, and I'll write out the gist of exactly what she said for everyone's benefit."

"Yes I do want you to sit down and fill in all the blanks!" Harcourt agreed. "Here is our transcript of what you said to refresh your memory. We really need to understand what's going on." She handed Sam a holo-chip. "Please don't leave anything out—especially if you think we might not want to hear it! We can reconvene later this evening and then decide what to do."

The report took Sam longer than she was expecting, and she resisted the urge to edit the exchange with Leila, since it seemed to have raised more questions than it provided answers. The obscurity was not lost on Harcourt when she and Byron met with her once again, having had the chance to read the complete transcript.

"What exactly did Leila mean when she suggested we would be more effective in conducting the spying activities of this Alien City for them?"

"Leila implied that it would be much less likely that a human presence such as mine would escalate the situation into a far wider conflict with the Aggressives, but I think she also meant that it would be easier for us to understand their reasoning once we begin this mission."

"Can we really trust that this Leila represents a different alien Nest? How can we be sure that she or they aren't just the same as the aliens in Alien City and are all a threat to us humans," Harcourt pondered.

"Yes that has occurred to me. But so far there's no evidence that the Nest are involved in the horrific activities we've learned from the victim we recovered. If I go on this mission it will confirm what that one witness told us, and hopefully lead to ways of stopping what the Aggressives are up to. If Leila's Nest helps us negate their powers, surely that should lend some confidence in their intentions?"

"Maybe we are being naïve about this Sam," said Harcourt. "We should not underestimate how sophisticated and unknowable they seem to be. Alien City could easily be part of a ruse to build up our trust and strengthen our belief that there is another Nest with far less attractive plans for us—all part of a clever strategy to ingratiate themselves to us."

"My take is that we cannot avoid looking further into Alien City," said Byron. "Whoever's pulling the strings has to be stopped. While I am concerned for her safety, if Sam's ready to run with this mission, then let her. She's extremely capable and probably has as good a chance of success as any of us, particularly given this offer of extra-terrestrial reinforcements."

"Thank you Byron." Sam's voice betrayed genuine surprise that for once her partner had shown concern and given her this show of confidence. While they had both held similar positions at UFODD, she had always got the impression that Byron either underestimated her abilities, or didn't understand her.

Rodney Jensen

"Leila gave me a brief history of how their Nest came about, and said that they evolved millions of years before our own civilisation started. She remarked that it would be more effort than it's worth for us to try to understand their reasoning and plans for us. On the other hand, even if you do think it naïve of me to believe their objectives are benign, the fact is that we are being forced to take sides, whether we like it or not."

"Maybe we're more important to them than you think," said Byron. "That guy who died before he could explain what he meant, seemed to be hinting that Alien City is experimenting with robot-human hybrids. It certainly ties in with the reports I've been reading of wholesale abductions from many nearby properties in this region."

"Look, we now have clear evidence that at least one and possibly two extra-terrestrial intelligence networks are taking an interest in our planet. But maybe the question is what can an intelligence network do without a means of implementing its aims?" Byron pondered.

"You mean some form of animate life such as humans?" said Sam.

"Two things, I think," said Byron. "Firstly, our planet has environmental conditions supporting the evolution of life. More importantly, it now has a population of intelligent life forms. It must be the combination of those factors that is what they're after."

"And the reason you think that they are after us humans is?"

"They may need agents to implement the mechanics of their nest system. Things it can't exist without. For example it needs sources of energy, presumably stars, and it needs the infrastructure to capture it."

"Including intelligent robots?"

"Yes I suppose that is how this all started, before going terribly wrong! The Sens report said as much—the Nest was born from biological intelligence like us. But then it became cleverer than its creators. There was a revolution, and from that point onwards artificial intelligence had a means to continue indefinitely refining its intelligence and self-replicating without the need for biological life at all."

"So what is it that you think they see in us? Wouldn't it be better for them to find an unoccupied planet? One with no competition? Purely relying on mechanical agents?" Harcourt pressed Byron.

"Intelligent slave labour!" Byron said.

"Simple as that?" Sam asked.

"Yes as pragmatic and simple as that," Harcourt agreed. "I've decided that despite many concerns, we cannot ignore the presence of Alien City and its activities. I'm intending to prepare Sam to penetrate the place and report back to us what is going on there. I'm hoping that the Nest will also be monitoring Sam's movements and protect her if things get sticky."

"You up for this Sam?" asked Byron.

Sam nodded. "It's what we've been trained for, what's expected of us. The reality is … I'm expendable, but the world isn't. You can be sure I'm going in with my eyes wide open. Not much more to say is there?"

Rodney Jensen

Sam agreed to attempt infiltrating Alien City, masquerading as a pandemic refugee with only her survival skills to rely on. During the next few days, she was put through problem-solving and training exercises to assist her in the challenge she was facing. Each morning she endured rigorous training in self-defence by a nuggetty expert in martial arts. He showed her how to deal with weapons-carrying opponents, reinforcing training that she had first learned as a rookie when she'd originally been inducted into UFODD. She was also armed with a deadly laser-blaster concealed in one of her boots. Byron was assigned to monitor her journey into Alien City via an embedded tracker and sending in emergency back-up and supplies as necessary.

Alex Whitby, UFODD's IT specialist checked out the special holo-link Leila had transmitted to Sam during her interview. She downloaded an extremely large data file, including instructions on how to open the necklace that the fugitive from Alien City had been wearing. When Alex handed Sam the necklace and invited her to put it on, she explained, "it turns out, the three dimples on the back of the necklace enable the entry of simple codes that lock and unlock it: three presses on the central button sets the device ready for data entry, then from left to right four presses, one press and seven presses. The same press sequence toggles the device from locked to unlocked state. We have no idea of how the device works, but we have tested it successfully, first removing the necklace from the victim, then re-attaching it. So we can be confident that you'll be able to remove it, if and when you need to."

"And now I'm the dummy." said Sam, what happens if the Aggressives change the code?" Alex shrugged her shoulders.

CHAPTER 6

Sam scrambled out of the ATGEV [all terrain ground-effect vehicle] in the pre-dawn light of the desert many kilometres from UFODD's headquarters. She was barely recognisable as the person who'd arrived there a week earlier. Her skin was stained light brown and roughened with cosmetic lesions, scars and angry moles. Her tousled hair, patched and faded clothes, her fingers and nails roughened and broken, belonged to a vagrant surviving each day with no tomorrow.

She paused to check that the necklace-device she wore was still shining green—in its safe mode. It was with great reluctance that she had agreed to wear it knowing it could kill her if it reverted to malign alien control.

As she walked further and further from the place she'd been dropped off, she began to see a faint discontinuity on the horizon ahead, which gradually resolved into a mountain range jutting out of the flat plain.

She remembered some recent UFODD advice: "We've scanned this whole area out to 50 km from here, much further than that victim is likely to have been able to walk in this heat," one of the remote-sensing staff had explained. "There's nothing resembling a camp or settlement of any kind, although this general area has been associated with quite a few UFO sightings recently."

"Nothing at all?"

The man pointed with the cursor he'd been doodling with. "That formation there appears to be more vegetated than other parts, and looks like it may be an ancient crater of some kind. But there's no sign of anything other than natural geology." He paused, obviously not wanting to commit strongly to something he'd been chewing over. "But I suppose if I'd wanted to conceal any sort of new installation I'd choose a place like that rather than flat plains.

Sam didn't like it at first sight; the distant range seemed a tenuous basis to be dropped from an ATGEV into remote desert country. However, as she grew closer, it increasingly felt like a good hiding place for something else. The formation seemed like it did not belong in terms of geological history. Her work mate's suggestion that it was the surround to an ancient crater seemed increasingly plausible.

Perhaps it was formed from the cataclysmic impact of an asteroid, she mused. Her pulse quickened at the prospect she really was venturing into Alien City territory.

Once she had walked to within a few kilometres of the mountain range, the track she had been following started to curve gently, running parallel to an almost dry creek line. From the direction the water was trickling, it seemed to come from the crater.

She found herself entering a narrow defile, the sides of which towered over her. She paused for a moment to look more closely at the cliff walls and up into the intense blue-black skies above. She spotted a large eagle, effortlessly gaining height in the thermal air currents, its beauty combining mastery of flight and ruthless threat to ground-based prey. *Probably on the lookout for a stray kid,* she mused. She could see herds of goats foraging for grass above her. A few were nonchalantly perched on a rock outcrop surveying the scenery. They seemed oblivious to the threat, then suddenly one turned its head in alarm and clattered off along an invisible path, the others galloping in hot pursuit.

The canyon track ran for several hundred metres further in, along a straight path, before winding again into a huge park-like natural basin. From her entry point she could see stands of ancient red gums lining the creek on her left side. The way ahead was surrounded by dense scrub effectively forming a tunnel and blocking any distant views to the perimeter of the crater.

Without having a clearer idea of where she was going, feeling hemmed in and uneasy about proceeding further, she decided to climb up the escarpment behind her to get a better look at the surroundings. She found a place to leave most of her bulky supplies and packed them under a cairn of rocks covered in branches. Then she set off carrying only her water, a small food pack and the laser weapon hidden in her boot.

It was a difficult scramble over loose scree in many spots, and as she ascended higher, the way was becoming increasingly blocked by massive smooth faced boulders. At one point, achingly close to the summit, the way up seemed impossible and it was time to turn back. But she was startled to realise that she was being watched by a large inquisitive goat standing on a ledge just above her. It gave her fresh determination to continue, and looking more closely at the rock face, she saw a small fissure at waist height with a rock projection above she could just reach. Hauling herself to gain a toe hold in the fissure she found she could then reach the ledge. It surprised the goat, which skittered off, showing her an easy route the rest of the way.

She finally found herself on a sloping rock platform just below the top of the cliff face. The view from her new vantage point was magnificent and she could clearly see the roughly circular form of the escarpment defining the edges of the ancient crater. She estimated that it was some six kilometres across and would take her the rest of the day to reach the opposite side by walking along the edge. She settled herself comfortably, chewed on a dry biscuit and took a sip of water, broke out some rations from her pack and used her electronic viewer to scan the whole area carefully. Yet she saw nothing of particular interest.

Then suddenly out of the corner of one eye she noticed a strange craft. It had appeared from nowhere, and was now hovering over a high point along the crater wall. It was an elongated box-like shape, resembling a very long, black painted freight container. It remained for a few moments before rising a few metres and then accelerating upwards in a northerly trajectory towards the sun, vanishing from view in seconds. Already, another similar craft had emerged from the hidden exit point and begun executing the same manoeuvre. She checked her chrono, and watched as more vehicles followed the same departure pattern at three minute intervals.

Rodney Jensen

Then something else caught her attention. Sited close to where the strange craft were taking off, but under the lee of the cliff, a very large array of what looked like receptors of some sort lay hidden from overhead view. Through her viewer she could see that they were mounted so as to face the sun square on, and after a while realised they were moving slowly to maintain their aspect. While they seemed to have a possible purpose of capturing or monitoring solar energy, they were like no others she had seen before. The receptor surfaces had an absolute blackness, as impenetrable as the space behind an open window on a bright day.

That odd looking craft and those solar receptors do not belong in the mid-21st Century. This must be Alien City. Sam decided to remain where she was until nightfall before taking a closer look at the solar array and attempting to locate the entrance to this alien base. She settled down in the shade of a bush and dozed off.

She slept through the approach of a squad of uniformed guards creeping up on her from behind. She was rudely awoken by a painful jab to her right kidney. She jumped into alertness, foolishly prepared to take on the nearest of the group, his arm raised about to hit her again with what looked like a short section of black pipe. Instead her survival skills came to the fore, as she realised there was no chance of escape from the detail of five guards. Each of them stared at her with an emotionless expression. She had little doubt that they would not care a jot whether she was taken dead or alive.

"You do not belong here," one of them, apparently their leader, stated with no intonation in his voice.

"I am bush-walking in these mountains. You have no right to touch me!" she blustered.

The man ignored her outburst. "Come with us. This is a prohibited area. You will be scanned and the data in your holder will be checked. We do not believe this explanation. The matter has been referred to our head of security for approval to terminate you."

He waved his weapon at her to get up. She realised with certainty that he and his squad were sophisticated andronics.

She had first heard the term 'andronic' (*Android-bionic hybrids*) during the two year period she was first inducted into UFODD. In the 50 years prior to the Great Pandemic, there had been considerable developments in merging biological functions with mechanical aids, including limbs and various other prosthetic devices. Experiments of this type were mostly reserved for last resort cases where no other options were available. The most challenging feat of synthesising vision, including a digital retinal array almost matching the ability of a normal human eye, remained elusive. Similarly, work on integrating brain functions with synthetic memory and external processors to achieve inconceivable extensions of life, indeed, the prospect of a fully functioning andronic with equal or improved capabilities to a standard human was still a long way off, as far as she knew.

In the wake of the Pandemic, such research was abandoned to the higher priority of stark survival. It was therefore a shock to be suddenly confronted by a group of andronics looking decades ahead of what had been previously achieved.

It had taken her a while to detect *any* aspect of non-biological integration in the guards. Sam realised what made her so sure, once the leader had spoken to her, was an absence of empathy and a coldness that was not human, surely a synthesised being, some *thing*, with an extremely limited understanding of human needs or reasoning.

The detail escorted her along the goat track she had already spotted from below. The goat track opened out to a wider pathway and Sam noticed a dense thicket of scrub ahead, slightly greener than the arid surroundings. The pathway became a wide descending ramp leading to some form of underground complex, with the thicket apparently planted on its flat roof, clearly intended to camouflage what might otherwise be seen from above.

They marched down the ramp arriving at an aircraft hangar sized door, which slid silently into the side of the embankment at a touch by one of the guards.

He turned to Sam and prodded her to enter the complex. As her eyes adjusted to the indoor light level, she could see long lines of the same freight container-like craft she had first spotted taking off in the distance. She was disconcerted to notice that they were floating about 60 cm above the floor with no apparent support. Each container was slowly moving forward in unison towards a patch of light at the other end of the cavernous space. Specialised robotic machines were moving around and inside the containers, as they slowly progressed along this alien assembly line. The robots were packing the containers with large components wrapped in synthetic material. She could only guess what they were, where the containers were going, and wondered if this was all part of an enormous effort to expand the Aliens' foothold into other locations.

The guards would not allow her to pause a moment or take a closer look at what was going on, but roughly pushed her towards a featureless wall positioned next to the entrance ramp at right angles to the assembly line.

As the lead guard approached and touched the wall, an opening the size of a freight lift soundlessly appeared, exposing a vertical shaft behind it. There was no lift-car or platform of any kind. The guard continued walking into the shaft without any hesitation and rapidly descended from view. The others followed pulling Sam with them. She resisted being pushed into what seemed like a sky dive without a parachute, but the guards ignored her struggles and brutally pushed her across the threshold into the abyss. She gasped, and supressed a scream, but controlled herself as she felt a weird sense of weightlessness. It was the same sensation she'd once experienced in a UFODD training tank, designed to simulate zero gravity using neutral buoyancy.

Sam noticed that the back of the shaft had a series of lights arranged in a triangular pattern of five rows, with one light at the apex and five at the base. The two lights in the second row from the top were illuminated as they entered the shaft and the third row came on as they slowly decelerated their descent and another opening appeared. *I guess that we must have entered the shaft at the second level, the first probably corresponding to the roof. If my guess is right, the complex has been excavated to include four levels underground.*

The guards manhandled her out into another vast floor area with a hive of andronic activity linked to sets of different assembly lines and manufactured components. As with the level above, Sam noticed that the whole ceiling provided even illumination through translucent panels and the floor had a soft resilience, similar to a sponge rubber insole. The parallel assembly lines stretched far into the distance, with very little noise, except for the intermittent sounds of andronic movement, fastening and inserting fixings.

Specialised robots were assembling what looked like large building components. At the end of one of the production lines, she recognised a piled stack of panels forming easily identifiable painted building facades. There was a range of panels, but predominantly what looked like the fronts and other sides of houses, some closely resembling building types found in Australia, and others in building styles she didn't recognise. They included surface painted graphics of mouldings and building features such as windows, creating the illusion of the modelling and shadows that would be found in a real building.

It gave Sam the eerie sense that the Aliens were engaged in constructing mega stage-sets. The overall realism was so convincing, it would be likely to fool even a trained observer. She wondered whether there were other similar bases like this one being constructed in as yet undetected remote locations. It was obvious to her that whoever was behind this clandestine factory had been going to a lot of trouble to hide the true purpose of its undercover operations. The amount and rate at which products were coming off the production lines suggested a possibly global deployment. She wondered idly whether there might be a set of Saharan buildings, or ones from the plains of Argentina? Anything was possible it seemed, given the thoroughness of this operation.

They moved deeper into the factory to an area which contained lines of booths brilliantly lit, like a series of small hospital operating theatres. In each booth she could see a naked human figure strapped to an operating table. A robotic 'nurse' was supervising some form of three dimensional scanning, judging by the shaft of green light moving across one of the bodies. A variety of sensors and probes were hooked up to their bodies including all the body entry points. Next to the scanning device, a machine was 'printing' out a series of body parts, some obviously identifiable as eyes and replacement limbs. Others, less obvious, included what seemed like new internal organs. A separate centrally located machine was processing assemblies of smaller parts—encasing them in a synthetic material, running them through heating and spraying processes, and allowing them to cool and to set, before finally being packed onto trays marked with coded addresses. The style of these modules looked like the necklace device she and the fugitive in the desert were wearing. *Maybe they're connected with neural enhancement and alien control?*

As she neared the end of the human scanning section, she saw a group of semi-naked victims herded together and seemingly heavily sedated. They remained expressionless at the sight of her and the guards, as though they were beyond caring. Suddenly one of them broke from the group and ran past her, dropping to his knees and holding up his hands in supplication to one of the guards.

Without any emotion, the guard pointed his black pipe at the man's head. There was no sound from the weapon, but he collapsed sideways like an animal stunned in an abattoir, hitting his head on the floor with a sickening crack. His eyes were wide open, staring lifelessly at the ceiling, without any tremor in his body. The other humans ignored what had happened, as a service bot moved into position, lifted the body, and dumped it into a hopper, joining others waiting for disposal or recycling.

One of the guards pointed Sam in the direction of where a group of humans had been heading. They were forming a long line leading into a darkened hallway. An entrance boom was admitting them one at a time, and they would disappear behind a revolving door. A low frequency humming noise was coming from behind it, pulsating in volume as the door rotated.

Maybe they're the ones who don't meet Aggressives' conversion specs and are being converted to food or spare parts, she pondered.

Her heart fell as she realised that she was being directed to take the runner's place. She wondered what it was that had driven him to his suicidal escape bid. There were only moments left for her to decide how she could escape. For he could have had little doubt of the risk he was taking. The telepathic voice of Leila suddenly cut into her thoughts:

Sam, listen to me carefully. When you reach the front of the line and are about to enter the door, you must drop as though you've collapsed. There will be an explosion within, which will blow out the door.

I've just watched one of these poor wretches killed! What do you expect me to do?

Before the guards fire their weapons at you, use the laser weapon that you have in your boot. The guards will not be expecting any form of retaliation, and will not know how to respond once they find themselves under attack. The confusion should enable you to complete the second phase of our plan.

Plan?

Yes to destroy this place. The Aggressives are intending to take over your planet, and this installation is one of their first steps. You have to believe us—they have no concern whatsoever about your future. There is a massive stockpile of energy beneath this complex. Your necklace contains a device that will destabilise it, causing a chain reaction that will destroy everything.

What about the humans left inside here?

By the time humans have reached this installation they are beyond recovery. Just follow the arrow showing on your necklace. It will guide you to the energy input store, at the bottom level of this complex, where you must leave it. It will inject a trigger signal, initiating the chain reaction. There will only be 20 minutes for you to clear the complex and get far enough away to have any chance of survival. There is no time left now to discuss this further. Cover your ears. You have 10 seconds left before the door blows.

Rodney Jensen

Sam only had moments to fall to the ground pretending to have fainted, before she felt the white heat and agonising pressure pulse of the explosion. She had deliberately fallen against the wall to one side of the entrance, to avoid the full force of the blast. All the guards who had been standing next to the door were thrown the ground. One of them looked badly injured with his leg making repeated flexing movements as though its processor had been damaged. Several others regained their feet, but looked out of synch, as though they were waiting to receive orders. Within seconds she began to hear clattering footsteps coming from the lift shafts, and realised that the explosion had stirred up a hornets' nest. *This time they'll be taking no prisoners,* she thought grimly.

"FOLLOW ME!" she screamed at the few humans who had survived the blast. "You have no other choice, unless you want to be turned into andronics." But as Leila had predicted, the effect of the sedating drugs had made most of them unresponsive. She pulled her laser weapon out of her boot and prepared to leave.

Relying on the indicator arrow on her necklace, she found herself returning via the same path her captors had used. No more than six of the other humans followed her and one suddenly fell as they rounded a corner. She dropped to the floor in an immediate reflex, waiting to catch whoever was responsible. The head of an andronic appeared around a side corridor. She took careful aim, the body jolted and collapsed to the floor. Several others congregated around him, thrown out of kilter by the unexpected resistance. She picked them off, one at a time. *There's more to come.*

"Pick up their weapons and use them!" she shouted at the other escapees.

She discovered that the black pipe weapons the andronics carried had a moulded section at one end and a press button she could activate with her thumb. It comfortably fitted into the palm of her hand. She beckoned the other survivors to follow her and picked her way carefully around the bodies, but there were no other andronics in sight. Coming to the next corner in the passageway, she peered around, immediately seeing a large group waiting in ambush. She took a pot shot at the nearest andronic and fell back, gesturing the others to take up positions on the floor, and wait for a renewed attack.

She heard their muffled movements before the first one dared to confront them. *They don't know how to cope with this situation*, she thought as she terminated him without any compunction. The andronics kept coming and the bodies began piling up. Sam and the others started using the mounting wall of bodies as cover from wave after wave of the guards. They seemed to have not registered the danger of continuing their advance, nor were they programmed sufficiently to take cover themselves. *This cannot last forever, there must be some higher level of intelligence monitoring what's going on?* The attack stopped as suddenly as it had begun, when finally, the wave of guards seemed to have given up and retreated. Sam waited as the sudden stillness continued for minutes before scrambling up and over the prone bodies, crouching low in case snipers had been left behind, waiting to pick her and the others off.

Rodney Jensen

She finally reached the wall where the lift shafts were located and could see no obvious way of making it open, and no other exit. *Holy Shit, we're trapped.* Sam felt stymied, but one of the captives walked past her, put his hand on the wall and an opening appeared as if by magic. *The Saints be praised.*

"Wait here and shoot them as they come out of the shafts, I have something to do," she shouted. She wasn't sure if any of the fugitives understood what she was saying. They were still looking so dazed, but the one who had made the opening nodded.

"I'll look after 'em," he said softly.

Without waiting to see whether he would be able to pump sense into the others, Sam jumped into the shaft and pressed the bottom row of the triangular display. As she descended below the threshold, she could see he already was leading them back into a corridor. *I hope he knows what he's doing.*

She reached the fourth basement level moments later and emerged into a low ceiling chamber stretching as far as she could see in the comparative gloom. The walls were painted off-white and the space was mostly taken up with what looked like an immense covered pool. Wafts of steam escaped from the edges. The atmosphere was extremely humid and smelled slightly metallic. A large ceiling-mounted duct emerged from a corner next to the lift shaft and ran about 30 metres until descending into a utility room located beside the pool. A catwalk beside the pool provided access from the lift.

You can hide your necklace anywhere in that room then leave immediately. Leila's voice broke into her thoughts.

Sam walked gingerly along the catwalk feeling the warmth of the pool and a tingling sensation on her skin. She spent a few moments checking for a suitable hiding place, finally choosing a spot above a cabling duct.

The moment she entered the code to detach the necklace, its pilot light turned amber. She guessed this meant it was primed and there was no time to waste. She ran out of the room along the catwalk and back into the lift shaft. She pressed the second row of lights to begin her escape, emerging from the shaft below roof level and running as fast as she could, and back along the rocky goat track. By the time she was nearing the place where she had first been captured, she felt a painful level of vibration and low-frequency rumbling like a massive earthquake. It was followed by an explosion and shock wave that threw her to the ground.

She was winded by the blast and took several moments to recover her breath. She scrambled painfully to her feet and looked back, seeing a fire storm raging above where the complex had been, and a gigantic cloud of black smoke forming high in the sky. Then she saw the figures of andronics in the distance heading towards her. It jolted her into flight, trying hard not to trip and making sure not to miss the point where she must descend into the canyon. She took a deep breath and began her scramble down the escarpment, concentrating on keeping her footing in the most difficult wall sections. As she was about to negotiate the high boulders which had once blocked her ascent, she looked up and was terrified to see the profiles of five andronics staring down, but not pointing their weapons in her direction. *Why aren't they following me? Why have they allowed me to escape? They must be acting under orders. The Aggressives must have a reason for wanting to keep me alive.*

« »

By the time Sam had retrieved her pack and found the way back along the canyon, out into the plain beyond, it was already late evening. The track was in deep shadow, and silhouetted shapes of rock wallabies and other nocturnal animals could be seen peering at her curiously from the surrounding bush. Sam felt an overwhelming tiredness and wanted to stop and rest. But she also dreaded what the explosion at Alien City might precipitate. Finally she decided to press a point below her left shoulder blade where her tracking device had been implanted. It set in train an emergency signal to UFODD Base, alerting them that she urgently required retrieval.

"Only use this as your last resort," Harcourt had warned her. "We definitely do not want to expose UFODD to alien attention. It's why we're dropping you so far from where we think Alien City may be located."

It was around 9.00 pm, as she settled down to wait and had almost drifted off when she began to hear the low frequency pulsing of an approaching ATGEV. A full moon enabled her to see its black profile and dazzling searchlight scanning the ground. It began to hover above her, slowly descending to the track, exposed to harsh contrasts of light and darkness. But suddenly the light blinked out. The barely visible craft seemed to be making erratic manoeuvres. Then, it spiralled out of control before crashing to the ground.

Sam raced over to the crash site. She found there weren't any flames from the crash or any signs of movement. Instead, as far as she could see, the whole craft was shrouded in an undulating black blanket, as if it was coated by a swarm of tiny insects. It had an overpowering and unpleasant chemical smell with notes of sulphur and gasoline. The swarm completely blocked out any sign of the interior.

In the sky above, a similar black cloud hovered and pulsated. Then after a few seconds, the cloud coalesced into a single spherical shape that moved up and away from her. It seemed to be aiming in the direction she was heading.

Sam felt a surge of panic. *We're up against powerful forces far beyond anything that UFODD has dealt with before. How is Harcourt going to deal with this? Are the Aggressives going to attack UFODD HQ now? I must head back to base on foot, however long it takes.*

« »

The same day Sam was on deployment to Alien City, Harcourt and Byron had been seated in the UFODD control room, monitoring her movements. Once she'd reached a position only a few kilometres from the strange geological formation, assumed to be her target, the signals from her tracking device stopped abruptly, and all attempts to restore contact failed.

Nervously rubbing her hands together, Alex Whitby had reported to Harcourt a few minutes later, "There's no technical problem at our end, we've checked all the systems and they're working perfectly."

"Doesn't sound too good for Sam does it?" Harcourt remarked grimly.

"Maybe the aliens at Alien City have some form of security screen that prevents signals entering or leaving their base?" suggested Byron.

"There's no evidence of that, definitely no jamming signals we've been able to trace," said Alex.

"If we're dealing with aliens, we can expect anything can't we?" said Harcourt dismissively.

"Ability to track our agent is a key part of her protection!" Byron exclaimed. "Shouldn't we try to round her up before it's too late? She's completely on her own. We can't just leave her there without any backup!"

"You're forgetting the Nest and their ability to monitor what is happening, aren't you? In any case, if we tried to rescue her it would blow her cover—and our own for that matter, which would put everyone around here at even greater risk."

"That's my wife we're talking about! She's not just a pawn in this mission. We've got to get her out of there and I'll lead the rescue party if need be," said Byron.

Harcourt pondered his words a few moments before coming to a decision. "That won't be necessary. I can't afford to put your life at risk as well. I think we should give her 24 hours, and if there's still no signal from her, we may have to vacate this base."

"You can't do that! She's obviously in serious shit. You've got to do something. We can't leave her there while we run for cover!"

"The alternative might be all-out-war. The possibility's been worrying me ever since we sent Sam out on this mission. Assuming that the Nest and this other Nest at Alien City are longstanding enemies, we have taken sides in what will be seen as a highly provocative action, once she's been sprung. The fact that her tracker has stopped functioning suggests that has already happened doesn't it?" Byron nodded reluctantly.

« »

Some hours later there was a whoop of excitement from Alex, who was monitoring Sam's movements before the signal was lost. "She's back on line," she said excitedly, "Wow! Just take a look at this!"

Byron, who had been standing nearby, looked at the 3D projection she was displaying, showing an area of bush surrounding a large stretch of sunken ground burning fiercely. There was a scramble of tiny figures and strange looking craft emerging from a hidden point along the ridge. It was like a nest that had been kicked in, with ants boiling out of it.

"How come we haven't seen this before?" asked Byron.

"It's like they've had some form of superior electronic camouflage screening their camp. I know I discounted that before. But maybe Sam's somehow been able to de-activate it. Must be connected to what appears to have been an explosion," said Alex.

Rodney Jensen

"It must be Alien City, there's the confirmation!" said Harcourt. "Look at it! It's right under our noses, we've completely missed it."

"It's a bit late in the day to have discovered this. If we'd had the proper intel, we might have thought twice about sending Sam in!"

"What are you saying Byron? We've done what we could to locate the base. Assuming that's it, now a smoking ruin, maybe it's because of her and she's achieved more than our wildest dreams."

"Maybe she has, but more likely it has something to do with the Nest. They're the ones who're pulling the strings. It's *their* wildest dreams, not ours by the way. And what happens next? Surely you don't imagine the Aggressives will leave us out of the equation now, do you? I strongly recommend we take a closer look to assess the damage and see whether they're already re-grouping. Drones would be a good idea, why don't we start reconnaissance immediately, while we still have the time?"

"I'm going to hold off on that until we find out more of Sam's status, ideally a debriefing assuming she's survived, and we can get her back safely."

"Amen to that!"

« »

Later that day, Harcourt came back into the comms area where Byron was still poring over the 3D visuals of the explosion at Alien City.

"I've been tracking someone who seems to have left the complex after the explosion. It looks like she's been followed by another group. It's definitely female and could be Sam. A few moments ago she disappeared from view because she's gone into a deep canyon and it's impossible to work out whether she's in trouble or not."

"OK. Let's assume for the time that she's ok," said Harcourt. But just in case she's not I'm going to put the retrieval crew on stand-by."

"There could be others beside Sam."

"We'll be ready for that if …"

Alex's voice cut through her sentence. "She's activated her emergency beacon!"

"OK get on it!" said Harcourt.

"Wait there's another message," she cried. "You'd better come and look at this.

Harcourt ran over to check the screen she was pointing at. It carried an uncompromising message:

You must evacuate your base immediately. We have detected a swarm that will destroy everything and you have no means of protecting yourselves from it. We estimate that you have less than 10 minutes to evacuate before being attacked. Nest

"God! What do we do now?" responded Harcourt without thinking.

"Follow their advice and run immediately. We must heed this warning!"

"I suppose so."

Harcourt was non-plussed. She wasted valuable seconds pondering whether she should do as Byron was urging. Finally, she picked up a red phone and pressed a button opening a PA broadcast, which could be heard throughout the Base.

Your attention. This is Director Harcourt. We have a Code Red situation. I repeat a Code Red situation. I am ordering all personnel to leave immediately. Do not wait to pick up personal belongings. There is no time. Your lives are all in grave danger. Follow the emergency procedures that you have been trained for. Leave the base and retreat to the outer boundary gate. We shall assemble there with all vehicles removed from the parking area. Do not delay. Go now!

« »

In the late afternoon, three days later, Sam finally returned to base. She was severely dehydrated, sunburnt and footsore from the punishing march home along the dusty dirt track. Only a few drops of water were left in her reserve flask. She sensed something was wrong the moment she entered the UFODD precinct. The inner zone gate, which normally required a security code for those entering, had been left ajar. She examined the security box to discover that it was covered by insects stuck to a dark black film. It had the same odour as the coating that had downed her rescue craft.

She entered the inner zone gingerly, but except for the buzzing of insects there were no signs of life. She ventured down the entrance ramp into near darkness, with only amber security lights to show her the way. The car park was empty but for the vehicle that Byron and she owned. Looking more closely she discovered a note attached to the windshield. Her heart thumping, she opened the note and read:

Sam do not go any further. Get out of here immediately. The Aliens have attacked the Base and all personnel have evacuated. We intend to re-group at our property and will wait for you there. Byron 21:00 hrs 04/03/2042.

She noted that the date and time were the same evening when she had departed Alien City, three days before. Having witnessed the effect of a swarm on the retrieval crew, Sam drove out of the underground complex without any further delay. She drummed her fingers on the steering wheel having chosen to use manual override. She was dreading the prospect of facing another swarm. It had become obvious that no Earthly systems of defence could ward off this overpowering alien technology. The remaining inhabitants of the planet were exposed and vulnerable. She put such thoughts aside as too difficult to cope with for the time being.

Having left the first entrance gate behind, she turned to the east towards her property. The road was straight and virtually flat and she had been driving carefully for nearly half an hour, watching for signs of renewed attack in the darkening skies, when she at last saw the outlines of vehicles in the distance. They appeared to be stationary and as she got closer her heart quickened. Another unfolding disaster greeted her. The vehicles were scattered around the road and one was on its side. *A forlorn attempt to evade attack?*

There were no signs of movement, no lights anywhere. All the vehicles appeared to have the same impenetrable black coating that had terminated her rescue craft and crew.

Rodney Jensen

She stopped her MAG 50 metres from the closest vehicle and got out, immediately gagging as the strong smell of swarm filled her nostrils. It was underlain by other sickening odours—burnt flesh and human decay. She could now see carrion eating birds circling above and some perched on vehicles trying to peck their way into the smallest openings. Gagging at the smell, she fumbled in the back of her MAG for her emergency supplies, at last finding a face mask. She put it on, then ventured down the road.

Close up the scene was worse than she could have imagined. The lifeless bodies of her former friends and colleagues seemed frozen in their evasive positions with no possibility of escape. As she had been expecting but dreading she finally discovered the remains of Byron sitting side by side with Harcourt in the MAG that had been heading the convoy. She had to rip her face mask off despite the overwhelming smell and stagger away as she vomited helplessly onto the swarm-blackened track.

55

PART 2
Moving On
- 2042

Rodney Jensen

CHAPTER 7

Sam drove the deserted road back to her farm in automatic mode. Apart from a terrible sense of shock and anguish, she felt an abiding sense of anger, making it difficult to concentrate on anything else. She'd been lied to by her husband and used by UFODD. But Leila was the focus of her greatest anger. She'd been cleverly conned by Leila, purporting to represent a benign alien intelligence on the pretext of helping to save her planet. It now seemed inconceivable that Leila, with her superior visionary powers and technology, would not have foreseen the outcome of her attack on their adversary. They could crush any human opposition as easily as a bulldozer could clear an anthill.

She had no sense of time as she drove, except when the lengthening shadows cast by the sun gave way to a moonless black night. She finally let up her headlong speed, fearful of hitting kangaroos, many mangled bodies of which littered the roadside.

Dawn was breaking as Sam re-entered the property she and Byron had lived in for several years. Coldly stripped of any romantic notions that may have led them to purchase the place, it suddenly no longer seemed like 'home'. Reduced to cold reality, it comprised an ordinary sized tract of marginal grazing land with the half-finished transportable building that had replaced the original homestead. At least it was weather proof, but the kitchen and bathroom were rudimentary. Everything needed to be painted. There were only a few pieces of furniture they had salvaged from other places.

Rodney Jensen

She entered the main living room and could see vermin droppings and signs of her last hasty departure. She collapsed on the sofa, throwing aside papers and magazines that were still open where she'd left them. She was overwhelmed by the stark reality that Byron was dead and would never be coming back. Staring at her home through exhausted eyes her mind was racing—*What should I do?*—*Coming here was mostly Byron's idea. It never was a profitable farm—We've been living hand to mouth—How can I run it by myself? Should I even try?* She was assailed by doubts and sadness and then thought of the implications of the Aggressives and their powerful alien weapons that nothing on Earth could withstand. She suddenly realised that she had overlooked an urgent priority—*I must try to contact other UFODD bases and warn them of what has happened.*

She entered UFODD's universal emergency contact numbers on her holo, followed by her security key. The screen displayed a 'code not recognised' message. *Have the Aggressives attacked our other bases as well*, she pondered, but she had no way of finding out, and assumed the worst.

« »

Some five days after Sam returned she had an unexpected visit from her neighbours Jack and Susan Longbottom. They lived in a homestead 3 km distant from theirs via road, but shared a boundary much closer at the bottom of the large dam and paddock just 500 metres distant. She heard their MAG approaching that afternoon, even before she could see the cloud of dust moving up the driveway some distance off.

"We haven't seen you around since we noticed you'd got back and you haven't been round to pick up Buster. And the sheep in the dam look like they've been there for a while, some of 'em waiting to be sheared. Is everything okay?" asked Susan wearing a worried expression.

The last time they had seen each other was when Sam had dropped off Buster, her sheepdog, for Susan to take care of. Sam had explained that she needed to make an unexpected trip which would not suit Buster, and that she was unsure how long she'd be away. Sam didn't seem like she wanted to explain more and was obviously in a hurry, so Susan didn't quiz her and was glad to be of help. But now she could see clear signs something was amiss. Sam was dressed simply in a T-shirt and jeans, her hair was a mess and there were deep shadows under her eyes. She looked exhausted.

"No it's not really," said Sam. "Something's happened to Byron, and I'm sorry to say ..." She found herself unable to finish the sentence, leaving them to work out that the worst had happened.

Susan put her arm around her while Jack looked on awkwardly, arms crossed over his chest and shifting from one foot to another. Sam started weeping uncontrollably and couldn't stop. Neither Jack nor Susan was brash enough to ask for details, but Jack finally said sympathetically: 'Really sorry, if there's anything we can do to help, with the sheep or whatever, you know you can call on us."

The last thing that Sam wanted was concern and sympathy from her well-intentioned neighbours—people she and Byron had simply been on nodding terms with. She definitely didn't want to go into the circumstances in which Byron had lost his life. Taking a deep breath she said finally, "I need to warn you both that there are reasons why you should avoid the desert road. It's become dangerous. Please don't go out there by yourselves."

They nodded, and Sam realised by their lack of surprise that they were thinking she meant the 'new bushrangers' as everyone was calling them. The bushrangers' increasingly brazen acts and violence against unsuspecting travellers on lonely bush roads had become common knowledge. It suited Sam to let them believe they were the reason that Byron had met an untimely end, rather than trying to explain the inexplicable—an alien invasion. *It won't be too long before they find out for themselves—a lot of people have been going missing—soon everyone's going to realise it's something more than bushrangers.*

She took a very deep breath struggling to regain her composure. "Thanks Jack and Susan for your concern. This is a really difficult time for me right now. I can only think of my immediate needs—trying to get back some semblance of order. Thanks for the offer on the sheep, but if you don't mind Jack, I'll take a rain check on that for a while. I'm sure they'll survive another week or two and I've got more pressing concerns at the moment. But I will let you know if I need your help and thanks for the offer." She paused for a moment realising they were still hovering on her doorstep. "If you don't mind I won't invite you in, because quite honestly the place is a real mess. I'm very sorry, but maybe another time?"

The two still hesitated. Jack looked at Susan who nodded back at him imperceptibly.

"Sorry, but there's something else we need to let you know," Jack came out with it finally.

Sam stiffened at the tone he'd used. "See, it's about Buster," he continued.

"Of course, how is he, I should have been over before to pick him up." Sam said, apologetically, feeling embarrassed at her oversight.

"Sorry to say he caught a tick. And there was nothin' we could do to save him. He's in the back of the ute. We brought him over—thought you might want to bury him."

"Jack she's had enough on her hands! We'll put him to rest if you like, Dear," Susan butted in.

Sam walked with them to the back of their MAG where Buster's remains lay, wrapped in a hessian sack. *Shit! I'm crying again.* She grabbed for a handkerchief in her jeans and blew her nose. Then she lifted him into her arms. "I'll take care of him now. You've been so kind looking after him. I hope he was useful?"

"Of course. Great sheep dog. He'll be difficult to replace. I'll make some inquiries if you like. You'll need another if you're going to continue with the sheep?"

"Jack! Stop! It's not the time. We'd better go," said Susan. "We'll come again` if you like, in a few days," she said turning to Sam. "Looks like you need a bit of help?"

"I do need to think things over. Yes I've been neglecting this place, including the sheep, and this has reminded me that something has got to give. I'm just not sure what to do right now. But thanks for looking after Buster ..." she repeated, her voice trailing off.

"No of course we understand," said Susan, "we just wanted to make sure that you're okay and we're so sorry to hear of your loss." She turned to her husband, for support. "Come on Jack, we must leave Sam in peace now," she said to him firmly. He nodded, and the two made their departure without any further fuss. Sam waited until she could no longer hear their MAG driving away before she carefully placed her bundle on the verandah, closed the door and retreated back inside her house feeling totally overwhelmed and defeated.

« »

Six months passed. Sam remained isolated from her neighbours. Her only trips outside the property were occasional journeys to Bourke to barter things in the market for a few essential supplies. Most of her time was spent trying to keep the farm viable despite the harsh climate, lack of water and perennial maintenance problems. On this particular day she had just returned from a futile climb to the top of the windmill to take a holo-pic of a part that was broken. The stationary windmill meant no water coming out of the borehole—critical water for washing in the homestead, irrigating her home garden, and replenishing the troughs for her flock of sheep. The sheep had temporarily been given direct access to their rapidly evaporating dam, and they had converted the dam surrounds to a muddy quagmire of hoof prints.

The windmill was nearly 100 years old and constantly in need of repairs in the absence of any new replacement parts. That morning she realised that it would need a blacksmith to replace some of the linkages or at least someone more experienced than her at metalwork and machining parts. Crude technology, but about the practical limit available in this whole area. *That damned windmill! It's been out of action since Byron was alive. He was the one who'd strap on his safety harness, clamber up the service platform, and fix the beast. I wonder if there's anyone else I can find to do it, even a temporary repair. It ought to be replaced if times were different. But I can forget about a solar powered pump. It's just not going to happen.*

She pondered what to do, as she pulled a bottle of home-made ginger beer out of her ageing fridge. The fridge was yet another example of obsolete technology, but the only thing available. She knew it didn't make sense to keep it going, despite its incredible inefficiency, wasting her dwindling supply of electricity from her two remaining solar panels on the roof. *Everything's breaking down and there's a limit to what I can do by myself. I can't carry on like this!* Her negativity was becoming a mantra, and was beginning to win her over to the idea that she must make a move—a daunting prospect, raising a whole heap of questions for which she didn't have ready answers.

You'll never work it out unless you begin, her nagging voice persisted. She detested the voice, it pricked her conscience, reminded her of the horrific events that had ended UFODD months before. It constantly urged: *get off your backside!* She wished she could switch it off, but it wouldn't go away.

Rodney Jensen

Why am I doing this? What's become of the Nest? Why can't they help me? They put me in this mess. And what about the Aggressives? Why did they let me live?

There is a reason, Sam.

The voice of Leila startled her. She had heard nothing from the Nest since the attack. Their lack of communication left her feeling angry and resentful, although she did want to hear their explanation. You've taken your time, was all she could think.

For your own safety—the Aggressives have recognised that you represent an opportunity to infiltrate us—an easy pathway in fact—to us and to our plans. That is why they have kept you alive and it is also why we have been forced to suspend communications. To do otherwise will put your life at risk and jeopardise our chance of helping you to save Earth from them.

You're abandoning me! Sam thought. *Surely you should have foreseen this, with all your unimaginable intelligence and ability to forecast future events? What did you expect would happen if I was caught using your technology. Why couldn't you do it yourself? Now you've abandoned me and left me with no-one here to help anymore. Do you have any conscience about what you've done to me, my husband and all my colleagues in UFODD? Are we just tools so far as you're concerned?*

No! Our Nest thinks very highly of you. You remain the primary representative of your people in combating the Aggressives. If we intervene directly, the situation will escalate and you will definitely be abandoned should the Aggressives wage virtual war against us. We can only guide you from time to time in ways that cannot be detected by them. So we have decided to implement better security in our communications with you. In future our messages must be limited, and we simply request that you find opportunities to resist the Aggressives with whatever local forces you can find. This will require special arms to deal with their swarms and andronics.

What arms, we have nothing effective to deal with their swarms, Sam thought.

We have sent you new weapon files capable of being made with your own 3-D printing technology.

I cannot imagine anywhere's left with a 3D printer.

The printers we have in mind were used by many of your industries until the pandemic. We believe they must still be in existence somewhere. The files we are giving you include a data base of industries known to be using 3D printing processes in the past. It will be up to you to discover which of those will be able to assist you.

And that's it?

We can do no more to assist Earth until the Aggressives meet effective local resistance. Do not try to contact us unless there is critical information that you feel we should know. In such circumstances enter LEILA_MN on your holo device. We will contact you once we have scanned your reasons for calling. Now we must terminate all contact. It is too dangerous both for you and for us. Goodbye. Let us hope the news is better next time we communicate.

Well thanks for nothing! Sam banged her head angrily, feeling completely marooned and helpless in the face of Leila's unemotional responses.

Sam felt burning resentment that Leila was expecting her to take on the role of humanity's saviour. *They just see us as expendable agents in their grand plans.* If she ignored the Nest and tried to tough it out, she faced a host of practical problems, including lack of water and food, and the impossibility of farm maintenance by herself. It would be a prolonged, isolated and lonely struggle with limited reward at the end, apart from simply staying alive.

« »

One morning, after a restless night worrying about the future, Sam's thoughts turned to her water tanks. With some difficulty, she checked the status of the three ancient cylindrical concrete tanks that came with the property. They each held 25,000 litres when full, and lay to one side of the homestead. They were the only source of water for drinking and washing. To her horror, she found that all three tanks were less than twenty percent full. Their sides had spiders' webs of hairline cracks that had been difficult to caulk over the years. Brown stains over the faded white painted concrete made her realise that much of her precious rainwater had been gradually seeping to waste. And in the six months since she returned to the farm, she could not remember a single heavy downpour that would have made any significant improvements in their water level. *There's only a short time that I can survive here without rain. I cannot stay here any longer. I've reached the point of no return.*

Her mind now firmly made up, she visited her neighbours, catching them both at breakfast. "The sheep are yours, if you want them," she said. "I've decided to let the flock go. I'll be off later today, and I am not sure when I'll be back, but please feel free to use my grazing land."

Jack and Susan could see her decision really meant that she might never be back, and made only token efforts to make her change her mind. As she drove off in her MAG, Susan said, "I reckon it were that dog of hers done it for her."

"Maybe it were, but I reckon the farm's beyond her anyway, her husband gone and all. I hope she makes a better go of it some other place." Jack paused to reflect on what her surprising announcement meant for them both. "What do you suppose we do with them sheep now?"

CHAPTER 8

Sam packed whatever she could into the back of her MAG and uploaded a copy of the Nest files from her Holo onto a pendant she always wore around her neck. She had decided to head towards the Australian coastline. *It should at least be cooler there*, she thought. *Are there any real prospects of growing some form of popular resistance against the Aggressives?*

After a day of hard driving east via Bourke and Brewarrina in flat land close to the Barwon River, she arrived at Walgett as the sun was getting low. The town had degenerated into a grid of broken streets, encampments on open spaces, public buildings and dwellings in ruins. A building which had once been a Catholic Church, according to a faded sign, had lost most of its concrete block walls and was surrounded by a huddle of roughly made shelters, formed from tarpaulins and blankets thrown over saplings. The air was full of smoke from camp fires.

Several of the inhabitants stopped to stare curiously at her MAG. as though she had dropped out of the sky, but there were no welcoming expressions. The main street turned out to be blocked beyond this point and she was forced make a U-turn, hoping to find another way through to the other side of town. As this was happening, a gang of children and older kids tried to prevent her leaving, standing in front of her and banging on the windows. She put the MAG into reverse and backed up 100 metres before making another turn into a side street as the crowd had begun hurling rocks after her. *I'm not stopping here tonight*, she thought grimly, and accelerated away, making several wrong turns before finally finding a way out of the place.

She continued driving until later that night, covering a further 200 km via Coonamble and Coonabarrabran over lonely back roads, before landing up at the entrance to another small town named 'Quirindi'. It appeared to have preserved some semblance of order with its wide main street and a number of buildings still occupied. There were lights showing over a pub which looked like it must have originally been built in the 19th Century. It had a large sign over the front veranda bearing the name 'Miners Arms'. She entered to discover a large drinking space and several customers, still propping up the bar despite the lateness of the hour. A large man with a red complexion and full beard stood behind it. He was heavily built and looked like he was well prepared to eject any unruly customers.

"The name's 'Don'," he said extending his hand. "It's short for 'Donald' but nobody ever calls me that," he said sounding like anyone who did would do so on pain of death. "I hope you don't mind those fellas," he said gesturing to one particularly noisy group clustered at the other end of the bar. "There's nothing else for them. They scratch a living sifting tailings during the day, and blow any money they make here at night! Funny old world ain't it!"

"Tailings?" Sam had not heard the word before.

"There's lots of old workings round here," the publican said. "In the early days they found gold not long after the Victorian gold rush. Of course them early mining days are long gone. But turns out that with more persistence there's still a lot out there to be found in some of the old workings—stuff that was missed in all the rush—probably the only thing that keeps this place alive now! Full turn of the wheel like!" he observed philosophically. "Started as minin', later become wheat, now minin' again."

"Now what can I get you?"

"I think I'll have a beer, it's been a long drive."

"Come far 'ave yer?" Asked Don, as he drew a beer from the tap with a practised hand and lined it up in front of her.

"Quite a way," she said vaguely. "I just need a room for the night."

"No problem," said Don. "Would you like dinner 'ere tonight?"

"Let me have a look at the room first."

It turned out that Don was well suited to advising her on any strengths the town might have in terms of manpower as well as getting an update on what was going on around the region. Don was unaware of any places that had been overtaken by the Aggressives, although he admitted: "Some chaps was talking about the place they'd escaped from. We thought they was a bit weird and didn't take much notice, to be honest."

"It was probably no delusion. I've experienced it myself," said Sam. The publican looked at her with interest. "I wouldn't think someone like you'd be 'aving me on now, would I?"

"No, one of the reasons that I'm visiting your town is to warn you about the Aggressives."

Sam took her time to tell the story of how she'd uncovered a secret base in the desert, setting off what was like an alien reprisal raid.

"Strewth!" said the publican. "If this is all true, what can we do?"

"You and as many able-bodied men and women we can assemble must join in and help kick them out. They're not expecting resistance, since their weapons are so far in advance of ours they think they'll find us completely powerless. But now we have the means to stop them in their tracks and we have the benefit of surprise—that is if we prepare ourselves properly. Would you be willing to help us Don?"

Don had heard many weird stories, but as he put it to his long-suffering wife as he settled down to sleep in the early hours of the next morning: "I've met a few in my time but this woman's got a screw loose, that's for sure. I 'ad to humour her. She could have turned on me I reckon. Besides she's a paying customer."

"We've met worse," his wife said without much interest. She'd had enough involvement in the day-to-day running of their hotel, without having to trawl through it again when she was trying to get to sleep. *A little attention to her own needs wouldn't go amiss either,* she thought to herself, sighed a deep sigh of resignation and rolled over.

<< >>

The next morning a group of a dozen or so refugees were camped out on the hotel's front porch. Don had been deeply asleep and completely missed their arrival in the early hours of the morning, desensitised over the years by various dregs and vagrants comings and goings at all hours.

"Shit!" he muttered as he peered out of his bedroom window, "what's going on here?" He could see that the group was very mixed, with screaming women and babies and anxious looking men.

Don ran down the stairs, unbolted the front door, and carefully locked it behind him as he stepped out into the milling mob.

"We need help!" one of the man shouted. "We've got to get under cover. We're being followed and they're not hesitating to shoot us."

Upstairs, Sam heard the commotion. She ran down the stairs, through the kitchen, out into the yard at the back of the building where she had left the MAG, and drove off.

She tried heading in a different direction from the way she'd entered the town, and once getting into clear space and open fields noticed a dark shadow pass over the windscreen, blocking the early morning sunlight. She felt a sense of dread as she recognised an enormous swarm was coalescing overhead.

Having seen what one swarm had done to the convoy that left UFODD, she left her vehicle and scurried along a path that led to the river crossing she had just left behind. It was a simple earth compacted bridge over a narrow diameter culvert drain pipe. She made a snap decision. *I'm going to hide under the road. It's my only chance.*

The river at this point was nothing but an almost dry ditch with a series of clay lined puddles and a smelly trickle of water making its way downstream. She stumbled her way into the culvert pipe and squatted against one of the side walls in the darkest place. She waited for what seemed like an eternity, before finally hearing a strange low-frequency throbbing, sounding something like a machine buried underground. She remained motionless as she sensed the light outside the culvert becoming darker. Out of the corner of her eye, she could see a black vapour, pulsating and drifting. A thin tendril wafted into the culvert and floated in the space above her head. She remained frozen in her squatting position. The tendril curled and became caught up in a sudden gust of air and passed out through to the other side.

It was several more minutes before she dared move. Sam finally turned her head, seeing nothing but clear sky. She gingerly crawled her way back out of the culvert and looked very carefully in all directions before rising into a cramped standing position. From there she could see the surrounding landscape above the river bank.

I must go back to the hotel, and check to see if there are any survivors.

She discovered that her MAG was covered in the black sticky coating but otherwise still operational. She drove back along the country lane into the main street that led through the town as far as the Miners Arms. She wasn't expecting to find any survivors from the group after her experience at Alien City, and there was no sign of anyone. She searched the hotel, but neither Don nor his wife could be found. Even the hotel dog was missing. Then she glanced out of a window towards the morning sun spotting two elongated black

box shaped craft like those she had first spotted at
Alien City. They were banking and heading west
quickly disappearing from view. *Another freight-load of
victims off to the processors,* she thought grimly.

« »

A lumpy mattress and rock-hard pillow did little to
help Sam relax the following night in Scone. The town
was quiet, and the hotel quite similar to the one she
had stayed at in Quirindi. It was a big step above the
degraded and demoralised atmosphere of Walgett. The
publican's wife explained: "most of the rooms have
been closed off, see. It's just me and my husband these
days. We don't get many wanting to stay here."

Sam suspected that it was the only room the hotel
had available for guests. Ruminating over the recent 24
hours as she tried to sleep, she kept recycling nagging
questions over her recent near-death experience. *Why
did the swarm ignore me in the culvert? Was it under orders to
let me escape? Was it a veiled threat? Are the Aggressives
monitoring all my movements, or was it just a coincidence that I
happened to be in town on the day of their attack?*

She could not help fearing the worst, while her
rational side argued that the swarms were becoming
bolder by the day, terrorising most the towns in an ever
widening arc from Alien City. That possibility seemed,
if anything, worse than the threat that she was
constantly under. *At this rate it's not going to be long before
they'll have reached the coast.*

She finally drifted into sleep, troubled by violent
dreams. She woke up early, and having paid in advance,
left without bothering to sample the hotel's self-service
breakfast room.

Back on the road again, she felt better and more confident. *I've met a swarm, I may meet one again. I need a weapon to deal with it next time. Now I must focus on finding local people, people who are also willing to sacrifice their lives combatting the Aggressives. I need to find a way to make the special weapons Leila described. My best chance of achieving this must surely be in Sydney.*

She continued eastwards towards the high mountains of the Barrington Tops, which slowly began to take shape as a faint blue smudge on the horizon. Out of curiosity she chose an even narrower road at the next junction and headed a few kilometres along its rutted and potholed surface before finding herself in the midst of a dense Eucalyptus forest. As she turned a corner, the road opened out into a long straight section and she could see a mountain escarpment ahead. With a frisson of excitement, she saw signs of a settlement with a plume of smoke emerging from above the trees, well below the ridge line. *I've finally found a place that looks more promising.*

It was around noon and she was careful not to repeat her mistake of travelling directly into an isolated settlement in her MAG. It was attention she could do without, making her feel far too exposed and vulnerable. She decided to find a place to hide it under cover of some trees down a disused track. She then set off the rest of the way on foot.

As it turned out, it took her far longer than she had expected to walk up the increasingly steep track, made harder by the weight of provisions she was carrying in her old pack. The place was occupying an enlarged forest clearing. She stayed where she was for a while, well out of sight, observing what was going on. Most houses had a homespun look, like they had been recently constructed from felled timber. The smoke she had spied from a distance was coming from several of the roofs, with the distinctive smell of charred meat and burning wood. Another larger cloud of dark smoke was coming from somewhere to the rear of the clearing, snugly-sited under the cliff side of the mountain range.

She saw that solar energy was being used from several arrays of solar absorbers haphazardly placed and angled to capture the sun. She also spied a few vegetable beds. On the cliffs above she observed two windmills lazily rotating in the updrafts.

People coming and going were dressed not in rags, but in hand made garments of wool and leather, showing signs of ingenuity if not great fashion sense. There were many children who were far more curious and playful than fearful. Above all, welcome were the sounds of laughter she'd not experienced for many months. It was as though she had at last discovered a new frontier, an independent community that was somehow surviving and growing, quite unlike anywhere else she had been until now.

She made sure that her laser was at the ready, stuck into her waist band in the small of her back, before penetrating the settlement. She could now hear the repetitive thumping of what sounded like a pile driver every 15 seconds or so.

"What yer want here?" A voice caught her unawares. She could not pinpoint immediately where it was coming from as she passed a line of small shacks.

"I'm looking for a place to stay," was her prepared answer.

A man stepped out of the shadows of one of the shacks. His face was bearded and he was wearing what looked like hand-made clothes including a kangaroo-skin jerkin over worn overalls. He stared at her without blinking with clear blue eyes. He seemed more curious than threatening.

"Got food or anything?"

"Not much," she said pointing to the worn pack she was carrying over one shoulder. "Just a few things," she said vaguely.

"Where did yer come by those?" the man demanded.

"Found some stuff in an abandoned store. I had some food but it's nearly all gone," she said, wary that he would probably try to check her story.

"We need more hands. Yer want work? We can give yer food and board in return."

"I'm used to hard work. I was brought up on a property." she said, embroidering the truth.

"That so! Cocky's girl by the sound of yer."

"Nothing like that."

"Yer not from round here, but. That's fer sure."

"What sort of work is it?" she asked, changing the subject.

"You'll see." said the man coming closer to her. Sam returned his critical look-over unemotionally, as he made a careful inspection of her face and neck.

"Been infected?" he asked finally, in a softer tone.

"Possibly, but I seem to be immune," said Sam.

"Hmm. That's strange, never heard anyone got infected and survived!" Sam was about to give him a suitable explanation, but held her tongue remembering just in time that she was supposed to know nothing about such things.

"I can't see no traces—maybe yer blood might be worth sharing," the man mused aloud, sending a shiver down her spine.

"Come on then!" he said. They walked along a narrow path between the houses. There was a strong smell of cooking which made Sam's mouth water. They ran the gauntlet of an irreverent group of kids who chased after them, until finally the man lost his cool. "Fuck off the lot of yer!" he bellowed. They ran off in all directions, leaving a few bolder and more daring ones to taunt him from a safe distance, well out of range of his fists.

"What's yer name, by the way?" he asked. "Mine's 'Serge'." She introduced herself. "Well Sam," he said," I'm just hopin' you turn out better'n the last dill we tried 'ere."

As they continued to the other side of the settlement under the cliff, the endless pounding crash every few seconds was growing louder by the second. They turned a corner, leaving the houses behind them and Sam could now see a dilapidated 30 year old landcruiser that was making the racket. Missing most of its body and jacked up so that one of the rear wheels was free to turn with the engine in gear. The engine was revving hard, but the noise of the overworked motor was nothing to compare with the repetitive crashing of the makeshift rock crusher it was driving via a broad leather belt. A large counter weight could be seen slowly rising to its highest point, before the locking ratchet released and the weight crashed down onto a pile of rock ore heaped in a massive iron hopper beneath.

Behind the crushing machinery an igloo shaped structure of mud-formed blocks served as a kiln. It had a hearth opening on one side, revealing a white hot interior. A crude chimney spewed black acrid smelling smoke from the top. A large balding man clad only in a singlet and shorts was shovelling chunks of coal into the hearth; his soot blackened skin dripping with runnels of sweat, from the heat pouring out of the furnace. The man turned, threw down his shovel and walked over to them.

"What we got 'ere Serge?" he asked.

"She bowled up out of the blue looking fer a place to stay. Looks fit enough to keep the hopper goin'. What yer reckon?"

"Hmm," said the other man looking unimpressed. He pinched Sam's arm above the elbow hard enough to make her want to cry out. But she ignored the pain, guessing that it was a crude way of testing her. "We'll put 'er on for a day—see how much good she works. If she's not up to it—then out she goes. There's enough useless mouths 'ere already without another!"

"That's 'Gem' by the way—this 'ere's Sam, Serge pointed his finger at his mate. Gem got his name from a lucky strike, or so he tells us, but we ain't seen no special talents since we've known the bugger!" said Serge.

Rodney Jensen

"Mebbe yer jest struck lucky with yer new sheila," said Gem with a dirty laugh.

"Fat chance," said Sam.

« »

Nothing could have prepared Sam for the endless stoking she endured that first day. Once the molten ore was ready for casting, with the help of Gem, her overseer, they had the difficult task of hoisting the bucket by a chain lifter over a series of moulds and very carefully pouring in the molten metal. She felt a sense of primeval fascination as an intense sizzling and bubbling sound accompanied the white hot melt, seething with sparks and flames as it contacted damp sand. It was difficult for Sam to resist reflecting that such processes had changed little in centuries and could surely be improved on. But she bit her lip, reminding herself to stick to her script of wandering opportunist-adventurer.

The only other relief she had from the endless routine of keeping the furnace alight was opening up the moulds a day later once they had cooled, to reveal simple castings, including axe-heads, blades and other basic necessities. Still far too hot to touch, it was obvious to her how important such simple artefacts would be. In an era when far more sophisticated products had all but vanished, it seemed encouraging that at least this settlement had survived the worst effects of the pandemic and was pulling itself out of the grinding poverty affecting other places she had seen. *But what a comedown—return to pre-industrial conditions and the best part of two centuries of learning and technology down the toilet. With UFODD gone where else can I turn to for a 3D printer? Maybe there's nowhere.*

She had difficulty straightening up at the end of her first long day when Serge finally relieved her at sunset, gave her some water, and took her back to her lodgings. She felt a sense of achievement in having lasted so far, although all she got from him was a grudging admission: "Yer done all right today, we'll keep yer on if yer can keep it up."

Serge led her to a small timber shack located to the rear of his own home. It had a separate entrance via a narrow path, and backed onto rainforest. Late at night the place was alive with the sounds of strange movements and animal calls she didn't recognise. They were to prove annoying come morning, acting as an effective pre-dawn alarm clock.

It quickly emerged that there was a shortage of food. Serge said: "The deal's to provide yer own tucker fer the most part. We're on short rations, but, and if yer want more, mebbe you'll have to find some stuff of yer own. Plenty of rabbits 'round 'ere, I'll show yer how to trap 'em."

After dinner, Serge showed her the nearest rabbit warren and how to set one or two snares along their trails. In successive days she never ran short of fresh rabbit meat, with plenty left to share around for other family stew pots. Sam never let on that her UFODD training had specifically covered the art of snaring wildlife and provided her with a coil of narrow gauge stainless steel wire ideal for catching rabbits unprepared.

« »

Rodney Jensen

Several days passed, leaving Sam feeling more at home, but questioning herself what her next step should be. She was curious to know how Serge had brought the settlement into being and particularly how he was able to start a simple mine and foundry—the one thing that might ensure its long term survival.

"Me Dad worked as apprentice in a small foundry Sydney way as a young man," Serge said. "They used to cast specialist stuff like brass propellers and the like when there weren't many places like that left. But Dad found himself on the scrap heap when it closed. The bloomin' navy was their main buyer, see—decided goin' offshore 'cos it was cheaper! He were forced to leave Sydney without me, me Mum and older brother. Come out this way and did it 'ard for a long time. Dad found work in a coal mine, and when we were a bit older we joined 'im near the mine. But me brother and 'im got killed. There were a cave-in." Serge paused and stared into space as he dredged it all up, misty eyed. It was a surprise for Sam, who was used to seeing his rough exterior.

Serge cleared his throat before continuing. "But yer know what, we all hated the Navy 'cos of what they done us. But it were the biggest favour we ever had— without 'em meanin' it. We 'ad to leave where we'd bin livin, can't remember the name now—'Ickville or summit – we come 'round these parts and none of me family got sick in the plague. We all survived. Can't thank 'em enough!" Serge chuckled in an amazing turn of emotion.

"How did you decide to start this place?" asked Sam, growing more fascinated by the moment.

"Ah that was easy!" said Serge airily. Not long after me Dad and brother were killed, the Inquiry decided to close the mine 'cos it were unsafe. Of course it were bloody unsafe! Everyone knew that. The shock of it all killed me Mum too. So I was left by meself. The only thing I knew about were mines and what I'd heard about from me Dad 'bout casting and stuff. There were a disused shaft round 'ere—but I reckoned there were both coal and ore there still. Just weren't worth the big boys diggin it up. I had nuthin' to lose, started real small and took a while to get things cookin' right. It were like I'd stumbled onto something successful almost by accident. People wanted to join. But I wouldn't say 'yes' to anyone, that's fer sure. Minin's dangerous. You got ter foller the rules and trust each other—no sweat. Which brings me to yer in particlar." Serge had his eyes fixed on Sam. She shifted uneasily, not expecting this turn in the conversation.

"I reckon there's a lot yer aint tellin' us. I'm no dill, and I watch the way yer doin' things. Sometimes I get to think yer could teach me yerself if yer wanted." Sam tried to act surprised as Serge continued. "Mebbe yer'd care to share yer story sometime, and then perhaps we can trust yer. If yer don't, we might have to let yer go. Unnerstan?"

Sam could only nod, not willing to take the discussion any further at that point. Over the next few days it left an uncomfortable tension between them, which she realised would only lift once she was ready to confide in Serge, leaving nothing out, in the same way he'd told her his story.

CHAPTER 9

Sam continued to resist telling Serge her full story on a thin pretext. *He's a very grounded practical man. How could he possibly believe in aliens? If I tell him, it may mean I have to leave here despite the hope I have for this place forming a nucleus of resistance.*

One day followed another. An uneasy truce formed between her and Serge. She could see he maintained his suspicions but had come to rely on the work she did, and sometimes the advice she gave him in an unguarded moment. But once he'd had a chance to reflect, it only served to reinforce his suspicions about her.

One day, Sam was feeling a certain contentment that her input to the foundry and mining efforts were making progress. The cast of the day had been poured, and the furnace was well stoked ready for another load of ore, when Serge decided to shut down the Landcruiser for maintenance. "The bloody drive belt's gone slack 'gain, and if I don't fix it, she'll shake the whole bloody pile driver apart," he said.

Sam was busy managing the area around the moulds making sure they were lightly dusted with sand to help slow the cooling process, when she heard a cry of agony coming from Serge. She dropped everything and ran over, only to discover him pinned under the drive wheel writhing in pain.

"Get me out. Get me out!" Serge pleaded in a very low voice. The constant vibration of the drive belt had pulled the Landcruiser slightly to one side, and in attempting to adjust it, he had brought the whole weight of the vehicle off its support tripod. The suspension 'wishbone' had landed on his left leg just below the knee. There was blood pumping out and Serge's face was white from shock and loss of blood.

Sam realised he would be gone in seconds if she did not act quickly. She ripped off her belt as she scrambled beside the wounded leg. "This is going to hurt." she muttered as she tied it around the leg above the wound and cinched it as tightly as she possibly could, while Serge groaned in agony. She screamed for others to come and help. Yet the mine was some distance from the houses, and nobody seemed to hear her. She scrambled from underneath vehicle and realised she had no choice but to leave Serge and get some more hands as there was no way she had the strength to get the wishbone off his leg.

Gem and another man had heard her screams and were running towards her as she started back down the path.

"Serge's trapped under the landcruiser," she cried, "he'll die if we don't get him out."

Gem took a look at the settled vehicle and then at Serge. His expression was angry and resigned. "It weighs a tonne yer know – can't be done quick 'nough."

Sam took another look at Serge. There was still a lot of blood oozing out beside the wishbone despite her makeshift ligature. She could see there was only one way to save his life, a choice that the others didn't want to face. She realised that even if they could lift the vehicle there was little chance that his lower leg could be saved. It was already practically severed. But unless she fully separated the leg and cauterised the wound he would die from loss of blood and shock.

"Get me the sharpest blade you can find. We'll also need a hacksaw. Put them in the furnace for a minute then bring them here." The men stared at her, shocked by what she was planning to do. "Now!" she screamed at them, "no time to lose."

As it turned out, the extent of the accident had made the operation on Serge more merciful than it might have been. When the men returned with a heat blackened hunting knife and hack saw, Sam found that the steel wishbone had completely sheared through the bone, leaving the limb virtually dangling on torn muscle and nerve tissue. "Hold him tight," she ordered her two helpers, and bending over the leg so he couldn't see what she was doing, she carved the blade through the flesh, finally severing the foot and ankle from the leg. Serge's molten groaning and writhing as she did this would live with her forever. With some difficulty, they eased him gently out from beneath the vehicle.

They settled him in a shady spot under a tree and made him as comfortable as they could. One of the men ran back to his house bringing back some sheeting while Sam put the knife into the furnace for another minute and prepared to cauterise the stump as best she could. Serge was still conscious, but only just. "Yer finished yet?" he whispered pitifully.

"Not quite," said Sam. "I'll be as quick as I can but I have to do this. You've lost a lot of blood." She took the blade and wiped it over the bloody surfaces, making a singeing sound as the flesh was burned and the wound sealed.

Rodney Jensen

PART 3
Quest for a 3D Printer
- 2043

Rodney Jensen

CHAPTER 10

Sam realised that what she'd achieved had turned things around. *He can no longer manage things as he used to, and he's going to have to depend on me more from now on, but I wish he'd stop thanking me and put it all behind him.*

She'd lost count of the times he'd repeated to her: "Saved me life yer did. Took courage. Can't thank yer 'nuff." It was always said in his customary gruff and taciturn fashion, concealing a ton of emotion, but after the tenth time Sam finally said, "Serge I understand, but it's what any decent person with the necessary knowledge would have done. Let's put it behind us now and start looking forward shall we?" Serge was taken aback, even hurt, but he never raised the subject again.

Once Serge had recovered from the trauma of the accident and Sam's field-surgery, he had fashioned a prosthetic leg with a shallow metal cup he had specially cast to fit exactly over his stump. It was held in place with a strap, and he used a crutch on his left side. He could hobble around, but as Sam said: "We need to do something better for you than your crude prosthetic leg—you'll end up wrecking your hips with all that pressure you're putting on them."

Sam's remark was a slip. She knew immediately it had fed his growing suspicion. "Like I said again and again, I reckon there's a lot more about yer than yer lettin' on. But it's saved me life and yer can keep yer secrets—it's up to yer. I can get around on me peg ok, but yer right, me hips is hurtin' terrible. What yer have in mind?" asked Serge.

Rodney Jensen

Sam had been thinking about how to craft a better leg solution that might help to bring back his mobility. She'd had a flash of inspiration: that if they could track down a 3D printer as suggested by Leila, it would serve not only as an essential basis for manufacturing new weapons against the Aggressives, but could also produce a more sophisticated prosthesis for Serge. It was quite a leap for him. "Yeah, heard the name, but it weren't used in the factory where me Dad worked. They was behind the times anyway. It were part of why he got retrenched. How they work or make things now, no, I 'aven't a clue."

« »

It was a cool evening when they were both sitting in front of a log fire after dinner and sharing stories, when Sam felt the time was ripe to tell him more about herself. She began with the time she had answered an advertisement inviting young people with a university degree willing to travel and have an adventurous career, and found herself at a UFODD training school in a secret base in the Rocky Mountains.

It took Serge a while to get his head around the fact that a serious international organisation would be chasing and supressing knowledge about UFO's. "I seen a few of 'em science fiction films like—but that's all they were—fiction!" he said dismissively.

"You're not alone in thinking that," she said "It's because nearly everyone thinks we're the only intelligence in the universe and wants to go on believing it, despite the weight of evidence to the contrary. It was for this reason that UFODD was formed. Its primary purpose is to help suppress the truth, because nobody officially in our government wants to admit that there are far more advanced civilisations than ours out there," she said.

Sam went on to describe how one of her class mates, Byron, and she were inducted into the Bourke headquarters for the SE Asian Region and almost immediately tasked with investigating sightings that were alien in origin. "There was one in particular, which is still classified, known as the 'Muldoon Incident'. It involved a prominent politician who was very publicly abducted while he was opening a new Aboriginal Housing estate. We never really got to the bottom of it. And in the wash-up, Byron and I did not have our contracts renewed."

Serge sensed from the bitterness of her tone that there was more. "I know what it did to me Dad," he said. "Losing his job at the foundry an' all. Never got over it."

"The flip side was that Byron and I were married and started a new life on a property not far from Bourke. But what I didn't know was that the organisation we'd both been working for retained him as an under cover agent behind my back. When I discovered his secret, I was devastated, but Byron and I never had a proper chance to discuss my feelings about what he'd done."

Sam then told Serge how she found out about Byron's ongoing relationship with UFODD when the organisation once more needed her to help them and agreed to penetrate Alien City. By this stage Serge's expression was incredulous. "Yer not avin' me on?"

Rodney Jensen

Sam shook her head, and blew her nose. "No. I wish it never happened. We were all incredibly stupid, daring to take on a force as powerful as the Aggressives, although we thought we were protected by the Nest. As it turns out the Aggressives destroyed the organisation I was working for along with my husband and all the staff that worked there and I've been on my own ever since."

While Serge was aware that some settlements nearby seemed to have been taken over by mysterious forces, he had assumed they were likely to be local bushrangers at work. "We keep well clear of them," he said, "there's rumours goin' round they come in—take control. There's no defence. The people in them places are slaves! You got somethin' goin'—we're in—that's fer sure."

"I'm still working for the Nest as a matter of fact, and that's where you come in. You see they want people like me and you to continue resisting the Aggressives. The reports are true," she said, "but what you don't realise is that these 'bushrangers' are being organised by alien forces. I've been given plans to make weapons that will be a match for them, but we need a 3D Printer to do it. I'm being straight with you about this now. The reason I came here in the first place was to help fight the Aggressives. I think we know each other well enough by now that we can work together on this. But first we must find a printer. Will you come and help me find one? There must be some of the old technology around somewhere. We've just got to track it down."

Serge was surprisingly keen to try to find a printer based on what Sam told him, even though he had no real idea of what it could do. He had developed a keen respect for what she had to say, and relied on her knowledge that it could not only produce weapons but also fabricate a far better solution for his missing leg.

Sam put aside the deeper problem of finding sophisticated surgical capabilities necessary to implant the prosthesis, hoping vaguely that the Nest might be able to help with that at some point in the future.

"Reckon the place I'd start'd be Sydney," said Serge after some thought, "but how're we goin' a get there's another matter."

"That's not so much a problem as you might think," said Sam, hoping her hidden MAG was still where she'd left it.

CHAPTER 11

One week later found Sam, Serge and Gem navigating their way along the old Anzac Parade through Kensington, towards the former University of New South Wales main campus. Their journey from the Barrington Tops into that part of Sydney could have taken less than a day before the pandemic, but by the time they finally reached the outskirts of Sydney, more than three full days had elapsed, delayed by complications from beginning to end.

As far as possible, they had avoided the former main highways as being too dangerous, not only from local groups vying for territorial control, but also more likely to be subject to aerial surveillance by the Aggressives.

Sam never felt that she could entirely rely on Leila's assurances that she would be left alone by them given the potential they saw in her as a conduit to the Nest. *Surely that cannot continue to hold them back indefinitely.*

So she warned the others: "We must travel by night with the headlights off and use back roads to minimise attention."

Travelling at night only made the journey more difficult. As they drew closer to the outskirts of Sydney, they began a slow process of negotiating a series of 'toll points' where some group or other was extracting a payment to allow them to continue through to the next one. Sometimes they paid in kind with a part of their supplies, but in others the demands were too extortionate, and they were forced to backtrack and take wide detours. They ended up coming into Sydney from the south because the old Pacific Highway beyond Hornsby was impassable and they had to turn back and skirt the whole Metro area, eventually to a point nearly as far south as Sutherland. For some reason the approaches to Sydney from that direction were less well patrolled and were not cordoned off, although the roads were in terrible repair and in some places built over with shanty houses. But there was still traffic of sorts, mostly on foot, a few bicycles and even horses were being used for cartage.

What had once been the main entrance to the University now resembled a very large open air market with stalls and makeshift shelters. The old academic buildings had mostly fallen into disrepair and the grand avenue that used to lead from the main entrance to the upper levels had been reduced to a narrow track between the ramshackle lines of shelters.

Sam had searched on her holo and discovered a reference to a 'Centre for 3D Printing' in the 'Faculty of Built Environment, UNSW'. According to the reference it been originally established some 30 years earlier. But the Holo-Net had become unreliable through lack of maintenance, and there had been no recent updates. Confronted by a university campus reduced to a ghetto and trading centre, it was obvious that the prospects of finding any useful equipment surviving were negligible. "We might as well find out where the Faculty used to be, having come all this way," she said, trying hard to keep the others' spirits alive.

Serge and Gem were none too keen on venturing into the bowels of the squatter settlement, where they would be vastly outnumbered if things turned nasty. But Sam thought that unlikely. "It's just a market for people trying to make a living. The risk has to be minimal," she said, wondering whether she was missing something. As she saw it, they made a curious group, one reliant on his prosthetic and crutch, all of them dirty and dishevelled after the long drive from the north. "Come to think of it, if we take a look at ourselves, we'll fit in perfectly I'd say," she remarked with a mischievous grin. She nevertheless made sure that her GX-laser was tucked in its customary place in her waistband.

The buildings were difficult to identify and nobody they asked had any idea what their former uses were. They found what might have once been a cafeteria now turned into trading store more or less centrally located in the campus and to one side of the main thoroughfare. They decided to search from this point to see if there were any buildings of substance left.

They had a breakthrough when they discovered a campus map on a remnant stretch of wall, mostly covered over with ivy. Sam ripped off the wiry shrubbery and wiped the grime away to uncover some faded text. She could barely make out a legend at the bottom of the map, the words mostly gone. But she finally found a partial reference "uilt nvir ment' and was able to identify where the building had stood from the map reference. She realised excitedly their destination was the large and long building immediately opposite them.

Sam's rush of optimism was only momentary once she realised that the building was derelict. Whole sections of wall were missing and windows were either broken or completely missing. The others were looking doubtful, but Serge finally said, "let's take a look, I'm curious meself now."

"I feel the same," Sam said, thinking out loud. "But we've got to be careful, assume that there might be people inside who don't welcome strangers. Gem you guard our backs and I'll go ahead with Serge."

They cautiously entered into a lift lobby with stairs running up one side. The stench of rubbish and human waste was stomach-gagging and they put cloths over their faces to alleviate it. They decided to walk to the top of the stairs and work their way through the building by coming down a single level at a time.

As they reached the top landing they were able to obtain a panoramic view to the south-west through a grimy set of windows mostly broken. "You can even see where the airport used to be, through all this smoke," remarked Sam.

"It's clearer than when I were a boy I reckon. But what we doin' 'ere? That wind's making me leg hurt like hell," said Serge irritably, as he stood hunched over his crutch, his free arm tightly wrapped around his chest to ward off the cold.

"Hello. Who are you?" A reedy voice startled them. An elderly man shambled out of the shadows of a corridor leading off the lobby. The man was clad in a woollen cardigan and flapping wide-cuffed trousers. His hair was thin and face unshaven with grey stubble. He peered at them short-sightedly through metal framed spectacles with one lens cracked and mended with an old band-aid. He looked and smelt as if he was in urgent need of a good wash.

"We're just taking a look around," said Sam sweetly. "I hope we haven't startled you?"

"Not startled, but curious. Please tell me your business. I have a feeling that it is more than sightseeing."

"You're right, of course. As a matter of fact we're on a quest," she said, deciding that the man deserved some explanation, with his educated voice belying his ragged and unkempt appearance. "Can you tell us anything about this place and head us in the right direction?"

"Quest? What sort of quest?" the man said with obvious curiosity.

"Have you been here a long time?" asked Sam.

"Yes, since well before the pandemic."

"Did you teach here?"

"I did indeed, but that of course all ended. I had nowhere else to go and I've been here ever since."

"Pull the other one!" said Serge, his voice abrupt and disrespectful.

"Well young man. If you don't mind my saying so, you don't know what you're talking about. I was a senior member of staff here and had access to stores which few others knew of. The area I occupy is well barricaded and I am able to monitor comings and goings from up here. Fortunately most of the people now living on this campus believe I'm a crazy hermit with supernatural powers, and have left me in peace, and thankfully able to get on with my research."

"Really?" said Sam with quickening interest. "Firstly allow me to apologise for my friend's impatience. His leg has been hurting him climbing these stairs. But I'm sure we'd all be very interested to learn more about the research you have been doing?" she said with a warning glance at Serge.

"I've been attempting to record the events immediately preceding and following the pandemic and the effects they have had on Sydney," he said, evidently pleased that someone was taking an interest. "But I fear that it's almost impossible to complete, because of lack of data and most of the people I could have interviewed are long gone by now. Similarly, I have no idea who could take over my project or which repository it should be left in, the world is so changed. I keep telling myself that what I am doing is a waste of time, but it keeps me busy ..." his voice tailed off.

"No! I'm sure that you're wrong," said Sam. "The world will never recover unless there are people like you left to help us understand what mistakes actually happened, what steps might have been taken to avoid total collapse ..."

"And avoid repeating them," the old man interrupted her.

"Look," said Sam, "our quest is to learn something about the work of the 3D printing group that would have been around during your time. Can you tell me anything about it? Or even more to the point, whether you know where we might be able to find a 3D printer now?"

Rodney Jensen

The old man looked at Sam in some amazement. "How did you come by such information, whoever you are? You're making me nervous!"

Sam laughed apologetically. "Please don't be alarmed, firstly let me introduce myself. My name is Sam, this is Serge and Gem's over there."

Having introduced her group she explained that they had come down from the country because of Serge's accident and they were hoping to find a 3D printer to make a better prosthetic device for his leg. "I found the information was still on the Holo-Net but it's very out of date," she concluded.

"My God! It's an incredibly long time since I ever heard that term. I am Emeritus Professor Steven Mayhew by the way," he said holding out his hand to hers, and paused to contemplate what she'd said. "Surely the Holo-Net's gone, hasn't it? I thought it's been inaccessible for many years?"

"Pretty much," said Sam. "I do have access to one of the few servers in which global data was held until the pandemic took hold, and remarkably I am still able to log in to it. But as far as I can see there have been no additions of any substance since then."

"That could be incredibly useful for my research. Could you tell me how to access this data base?"

"It may be difficult," admitted Sam, "Since it would be breaching the security of the organisation I used to work for. But maybe I might be able to obtain clearance if and when I re-establish contact. They are overseas as it happens, and I have been unable to raise them for over a year. It's not looking good, or for the US where they're sited for that matter. In the meantime, can you tell me about the 3D Printing Centre?"

"Well, you're absolutely correct. This Faculty used to have a special centre for 3D printing associated with the industrial design department. It was one of the most advanced in the Southern Hemisphere. But I fear that is almost the extent of what I know, since the technology of 3D printing was quite unrelated to my responsibilities."

"Can you show us where the Centre was located and what equipment they had then?"

The man's expression was regretful. "It is no longer there; long since taken over the by the many people you would have observed as you approached this building. If there had been anything of use it would have been seized, taken apart and traded years ago. Nothing like that has lasted. You must realise that, surely?"

"Yes, I must admit it was a long shot. But we need to find a printer. It's terribly important!"

"Do you mind telling me why?"

Because if we don't do something about my friend Serge's leg he will end up in a wheel chair and living on a country property in a wheel chair is nigh on impossible," said Sam, deciding to edit out the real priority until she knew the man better and felt she could trust him. But she seriously underestimated her listener.

"Are you sure that's all it is, not that I doubt the seriousness of your friend's plight, I can't help feeling there's more to this than you're telling me?"

Rodney Jensen

Sam drew a breath as she formulated an answer that might satisfy his curiosity. "You're right, but you will just have to trust me that there is an even higher and more serious reason, which I am not really at liberty to explain since it is a matter of National Security. If you can help us, we may be able to help you with the access to the Holo-Net I mentioned before."

"My God!" he muttered, "you've got me really intrigued now, but I suppose I must be patient." He turned away resting his chin on the upturned palm of his hand. He appeared to be turning over everything Sam had said to him, before finally coming to a weighty decision. "Can I come with you?" he came out with at last. "It's been a long time you understand, and I may be able to assist. We could help each other in fact. I don't want to die alone here. And I think maybe you or the organisation you say you used to belong to might be interested in my history when it's completed?"

Sam was taken aback, the last thing she wanted was responsibility for the care and maintenance of a frail old man in his late 70's with the likelihood of special health needs to come.

"I don't know, I'll have to ask the others," she said. "How exactly do you think you might be able to help us?"

"The thing is," he explained, "I used to be on a Faculty Committee which had responsibility for approving large expenditure for significant equipment. One of the most expensive things we ever purchased was a state of the art 3D Printer. As I recall, it was manufactured by a company called DELTEX and their agent at the time was located at a place called Macquarie Park. I could take you there."

Sam was blown away. "How long would it take you to get your things together?" she asked him softly.

CHAPTER 12

Accommodating Emeritus Professor Steven Mayhew proved to be far more problematic for Sam than even finding their way to DELTEX at Macquarie Park.

Sam was stunned once he'd cleared a way through to the office suite where he'd been holed up. It had book cases filled with publications in box files on all four walls and cartons of papers piled high on the floor, the visible part of which was reduced to a narrow pathway to his desk, also overflowing with paper.

"My computer gave up the ghost long ago, even though I had rigged up a power system to run it," he said pointing out ancient equipment including a large car battery, a DC-AC inverter, and obsolete desktop computer sitting on top of a pile of cartons in one corner. "But the virtue of paper is that it is far more reliable and permanent. Where would I be if I had put my reliance on 'the Cloud' as most did once, and too late regretted having no way of recovering all their valuable data."

Mayhew's attached bathroom-cum toilet was even more confronting. The toilet bowl, shower and washbasin, encrusted with years of accumulated waste and grime, looked like they had not been cleaned since the pandemic. The room was suffused with a stale noxious odour that left them gagging until they could open one of the hopper windows and breathe in fresh air.

By common agreement Mayhew would not be allowed to join them unless he had a comprehensive hygiene overhaul. "It's going to be a long journey and maybe you need to freshen up first?" suggested Sam diplomatically. "Have you got any clean clothes?" she continued, ignoring the look of consternation on his face. Mercifully, Gem took over the task of directing him to undress and bathe, having found a bucket in a cupboard and water from a standpipe outside the building. Sam searched his bedroom for cleaner clothes and drew a blank. In the end they had to wash out his clothes as well and wait for them to dry. While wrapped in a towel, Mayhew grumpily sorted through his papers and decided what to take in the single suitcase that he was allowed.

"The MAG's already full as it is," explained Sam. "Most of this will have to be left behind, I'm sorry. Maybe we can retrieve some of the rest later, but you'd need a trailer to do it, and I can't make any firm promises. We've got our own survival to worry about for now. But I hope we can come back for all this boxed stuff once the time is right."

Mayhew could see that the condition for taking him was non-negotiable and seemed overwhelmed by the enormity of his decision to leave his 'safe haven' with all it contained. He sat on a chair looking confused and helpless. "All this time," he wailed. "My life's work! What will become of it?"

Sam felt sorry for him and embarrassed by his outburst, saddened that she was forced into a position of such hard-heartedness. "I understand how you must be feeling Steven, but you've been here such a long time that the reality of the world as it now is, has passed you by. It's obvious to us that you cannot survive much longer like this. It's a miracle in fact that the others outside this building have left you in peace so long." Mayhew remained unconvinced until his clothes had dried, he was able to dress himself again and regain his dignity.

The following evening they set off towards Macquarie Park, Mayhew sat in the front seat, helping Sam to navigate a journey she only dimly remembered. "The Sydney Harbour Bridge is not worth risking," he muttered. "I've heard that most people heading north-west are now going via Ryde." However, that information proved inaccurate and the Concord Road approach was barricaded off, forcing them to head further west and then back-track through Silverwater.

Travelling in the dark, with only parking lights on, greatly increased the difficulty of avoiding stray pedestrians and the odd missile lobbed at their MAG from disgruntled survivors. On arrival close to their destination, they discovered that DELTEX Corporation unlike most of the rest of Macquarie Park was not in a ruinous condition. Its sign was clearly displayed at the entrance. The main building was sited amid large landscaped grounds of what had once formed the central part of a high technology office-park development.

A small old fashioned looking manager's box, with its light on, was situated next to the entrance gate. Within moments, a lone security guard appeared at the entrance. He was carrying a holstered automatic laser weapon and wearing a black peaked hat emblazoned with the DELTEX logo. His expression was rigid, unwelcoming, and his hand was hovering over the holster.

CHAPTER 13 The Story of DELTEX

It was 2015 when home to Hiram Rogers was Silicon Valley. The thin, intensely absorbed teenager was doing his best to ignore his mother as he sat hunched over a workshop table in the basement. He flinched slightly as she shouted, "Hiram what the hell are you doing, do you realise what the time is?" As he flicked his eyes up, he could see her standing at the head of the stairs in her frayed dressing gown, hands on hips, staring down at him. He returned to examining the component he was working on, ignoring her.

Rogers was a nerdy kid who'd just managed to escape bullying at school by using his wits and off-beat sense of humour. He had just one close friend, Lance, who could beat him at chess and help out with his math assignments, and sometimes come to his assistance when he'd allowed his loud mouth get the better of him. Rogers didn't suffer fools gladly. On one occasion, he'd only narrowly escaped ending up in hospital when he told someone at his college three years older than himself, built like a brick shithouse and star-member of the football team, that the only reason for his success in life was because he had rich parents and had been awarded a football scholarship.

That night Rogers was engrossed in the workings of the 3D printer his father had given him for his 17th birthday, wanting to encourage his curiosity and interest in new technology.

Jack, his father, worked as a security guard for a company in Silicon Valley. It was developing new prototypes including drones using 3D printing, and routinely replaced their printers once newer and better systems became available. All their second-hand equipment was offered to staff for sale at heavily discounted prices. One evening, Jack happened to be in the right place at the right time and noticed a 3D printer less than two years old had been put in the equipment store waiting to be sold off. It happened that his son's birthday was coming up, so Jack approached the office manager as soon as he could catch his attention.

"What do you want for that old DOLMAR printer in the storeroom, Dick?" Jack asked him innocently. Dick scratched his head wondering what on Earth his security guard would want with a 3D printer. "Planning to sell it to a terrorist or someone?" His joke was meant to provoke Jack, but fell flat.

"No, it's for my son. See, he's always been more interested in IT stuff than sport, and it's his birthday next week." The last remark was the clincher.

"Okay Jack, I believe you, thousands wouldn't. Give us 200 bucks in cash and it's yours. Just get it out of here when no one else's around. And," he added cautiously, "as far as anyone's concerned should they ask, tell 'em 'we sold it on eBay'." Dick tapped his nose so that Jack could clearly understand where he was coming from.

Jack quickly pulled his wallet out and handed over the cash, representing a fraction of what the printer was worth and could have still been sold for a lot more if the company had better control of its management practices. The printer vanished from the storeroom with the help of a friend's pickup truck and nobody in the office was any the wiser.

« »

The workbench in the basement had been taken over by Hiram some time before, much to his father's annoyance. That night the printer he'd been given was in bits, and Hiram was going through the service manuals he'd downloaded, checking out particular assemblies with the help of a head mounted magnifying lens and spotlight.

"What are you doing?" Hiram knew that his mother would persist until he gave her an answer.

"Trying to understand what's causing this printer not to work right. It's taking longer than I expected."

"Go to bed! You'll work more effectively if you've had a good night's sleep." Hiram took no notice. For the second time that evening his mother retreated in a huff. She knew that when he was immersed in something like this, she was wasting her breath.

« »

"Wow that's awesome! What's the problem? What do you want to do with it?" asked Lance.

"It is actually the 'how' not the 'what'," Hiram answered his friend cryptically.

Lance was the only one at college he'd confided in about the printer, on pain of death. What he told his mother, was actually a white lie. The printer was in perfect working order. He just wanted to improve it. Lance was a whiz at all things electronic. Hiram thought maybe Lance could sort out something which so far he'd been unable to figure out himself.

"I'm trying to improve the output resolution by a factor of 10."

"That all! If it were that easy, don't you think the manufacturers would have done it themselves?"

"Actually they sort of have. The latest model they're selling has five times the resolution of this one. It's really needed, particularly for the detailed assemblies. The only thing I've been able to discover affecting resolution from checking their manuals is the processor and memory chips. I'm hoping that to upgrade this model all we've got to do is change the chips?"

"Did you think of asking their service department about this?"

"Get real! Do you think they'd help me do a small mod which costs only a few bucks when the cost of their new printer is worth thousands to them? Worse, if the mod is really that simple, and it got out, everyone'd be doing it. Bang goes their new printer!"

"Not everyone thinks like you Hiram. Such an opportunist!"

"We're not all as naïve as you, you mean. You'd be surprised how many of me are out there! Take a look at the Net sometime. It's full of wanna-be inventors looking for cheap patches like this; sort of global conspiracy, to outsmart greedy companies like DOLMAR."

"Quite like the sound of that! But what's in it for me?"

Here's the thing. You know a load more about electronics than I do. If you want to team up and help me turn this ho-hum printer to cutting edge—then maybe we can go into business together?" Drones, weapons, bio-med gear—you name it—we can make it!"

"What *specifically* do you want?"

"Right now I need someone who can understand these machines completely and confirm what the differences are. And more to the point, what's needed to upgrade this one—the cheapest way possible. I'm hoping you'll be able to work it out with the manuals I've downloaded for you to check out."

"Fat chance! You seriously think they'd put their most sacred intellectual property into a service manual for God's sake?"

"Maybe not. But can you reverse engineer this one to understand what would be needed and how the chips used in the later model do it?"

"It'd take a while. Wanna give me a copy of those manuals and any notes you've made?"

"Is that a 'yes' then?"

"Suppose it is. I can't afford a lawyer which people like us are supposed to do. I mean, help us work out how we are going to share profits and protect our IP. That sort of stuff. You happy with that?"

"How long have we known each other? I'm assuming its fifty-fifty all the way! It's a trust thing isn't it?"

"I guess it is. But trust's one thing, keeping records another. Why don't I email you what we've agreed today, and we can both sign off on that. In the long run I think we'd both be better off with some paperwork don't you?"

"Sure! Go ahead. I'll sign. We're going to be rich!"

"Yeah!" Lance began to see a side of Hiram he'd hardly noticed before.

« »

It didn't take Lance long to understand how the different models worked when the user selected its various options. "They're almost identical as far as machine logic's concerned," he reported two weeks later. "The only difference is that the main processor is much faster, and the on-board memory is also hugely improved."

"Are the chips proprietary?"

"Of course they are. DOLMAR needed something that had specific functions rather than trying to make an all-purpose logic processor work. Besides that, all-purpose chips that anyone can buy off the shelf would make it far too easy for people like you and me to emulate their highly complex circuitry."

"So what are we going to do?"

"Tweak a processor that is off-the-shelf to do the same thing. Or, design one ourselves and have it made by a chip company. That would cost far more of course."

"How much more?"

"No idea, thousands of dollars I guess. And maybe a share of the action. I'm not sure."

"And what about the off-the-shelf option?"

Rodney Jensen

"Again it's something I've got to look into. I'm hoping to find an answer on that soon, but I'm thinking that it would also be necessary to build a simple interface board as part of the chip requirements, but that part shouldn't take so long. It's finding an alternative main processor chip on the shelf that's the problem."

Two weeks later Lance had asked to meet in a coffee shop they used outside college. He told Hiram conspiratorially over his mobile that he preferred to do it this way. But it was obvious he was excited and could hardly contain himself till they met.

"I realised that the processor chip DOLMAR uses comes from the same company that makes the processors for the SMEX hospital scanners. The ones that image your body as it goes into a tunnel. They're almost identical." Lance was sounding jubilant. "What's more I contacted their service desk, told them I was servicing a SMEX and asked for a replacement processor, the one that matches DOLMAR's latest model."

"Simple as that?"

"Here it is!" He pulled out a zip locked plastic bag with anti-static coating. The nondescript chip with multiple pins was nestled inside, mounted on a piece of silver backed styrofoam.

"Wow unreal!" The two smashed their palms together in high fives, in their excitement. "This calls for a celebration. When can we check it out?"

"As soon as I've made the interface I'll bring it over. I'm confident that this is going to work. The increased memory is easy because we can definitely use standard chips for that," said Lance.

« »

By 2025, the two friends Hiram Rogers as President, Lance Brookenheim as Secretary, Treasurer and CEO were in charge of the DELTEX Corporation, a privately registered business specialising in 3D Printing services. They had developed a range of revolutionary printers that no longer used the conventional process known as 'fused deposition modelling'. Instead they had developed and patented a truly 3D process known as PPA or 'progressive particle accretion'. Their top of the range printer, known as the DELTEX 500 Spatial Printer, used a neutral bath in which matter was suspended and accreted to form the growing model from nano-particles. The new printer had the advantages of speed, versatility and economy. The design was hugely successful, radically changing the approach to 3D printing in nearly every sector of the production industry, including space exploration, defence and bio-technology. Ultimately it earned them millions of dollars. The DELTEX Corporation diversified and grew rapidly, soon having a conservative market capitalisation of $US 3 billion.

That same year, Rogers was invited to present a keynote address at an international conference on innovation technology in Sydney. It was a terrific opportunity to showcase the revolutionary DELTEX printer. Attending Roger's address was a research scientist, Keith Donaldson, an unassuming former consultant mechanical engineer of considerable skills, who'd been appointed Head of an Australian Defence

Force organisation responsible for weapons research. As far back as 2015, the fused deposition modelling processes had enabled the production of drones carrying on board weapons without any need for a machine shop. By 2025 modern warfare was routinely supported by weapons with varying degrees of artificial intelligence. It was therefore no surprise that Donaldson would be particularly interested in the potential of the DELTEX 500 for prototyping new weaponry.

What Donaldson could not know was that the DELTEX Corporation was in a highly classified relationship with an Ivy League University back in the US. Its centre for bionic research teamed up with the US military's own weapons research division had commissioned DELTEX to make use of its advances in spatial printing to create a fully functioning humanoid fighting machine, code-named 'Zapper'. Zapper was planned for either remote control, or independent aggressive action on the battlefield. The second of these options was the most controversial. There had been mounting pressure from various interest groups in the United States over independent fighting machines which had proved capable of killing innocent victims politely referred to as 'collateral damage'. By 2025, drones were all too often inflicting un-planned casualties surrounding various theatres of war. The bionic research was kept under tight security wrap and the angry protests against use of artificial intelligence in warfare were ignored.

While Rogers was in Sydney, Donaldson invited him to a meeting with the Australian Defence Chiefs, to investigate the potential benefits of the DELTEX

500, including manufacturing drones. Hiram Rogers did not disclose any details of the DELTEX involvement in the US bionic research program since it was subject to strict classification, notwithstanding the Australia and US defence pact.

Rogers saw not only a huge commercial opportunity for DELTEX in Australia, but a valuable investment for himself and his family. The United States in the 2020s was already experiencing insoluble environmental problems with cities like New Orleans proving uninhabitable as a consequence of rising sea levels. Cases of mass civilian murder rampages resulting from unregulated gun ownership were a constant and recurring nightmare.

Rogers liked what he saw in Sydney and was particularly taken with the comparatively clean and neat ambience of Macquarie Park, a high technology industrial precinct. As it happened, a large site and commercial complex, involved in importing printers and cameras, had come onto the market. Rogers held meetings with some local advisers, set up an anonymous shelf-company and made an offer, far higher than his intelligence had suggested the vendors were hoping for. Within two weeks of the initial meeting the contract was signed. Rogers then talked his Co-Directors back in the States into setting up an entirely new arm of DELTEX centred in Sydney to service Australasia and Asia Pacific. It was a no-brainer.

Apart from making Rogers a lot of money in lease payments from DELTEX (a fact which he kept quiet and buried in a secure Bahamas-based tax haven) was the added personal benefit of a safer home—given mounting concerns with the environment of the United States.

Rogers took a keen interest in the architectural redevelopment of the site. It offered the company not only the opportunity to market and distribute its products throughout Australasia, but also the establishment of a new offshore research lab, complementary with DELTEX's facilities in the States and a significant backup in case things should go belly up there.

As time moved on, Rogers and his family had become permanently absorbed into the Sydney scene. He decided in 2034 to step aside from Presidency in favour of becoming Regional Head of Operations, Southeast Asia. It was a grand title which formalised his decision to remain at the Macquarie Park Headquarters indefinitely. In 2035, the global pandemic struck at a time when DELTEX was at its zenith, rivalling former giants like Apple, Media-Soft and Gen-Sys.

It coincided with Rogers' wife Tina and two children taking a prolonged break in the United States to enable Tina to go back to school and complete a special course for mature-aged students at Menlo College in Silicon Valley. It was also close to where their family home was located. In the ensuing chaos, all communications from America were lost. He had never seen or heard from them since.

At the height of the pandemic, Rogers was only able to survive with the help of one loyal member of staff, Moses Jefferson, an African American security guard he'd previously entrusted with his life on more than one occasion, including once when some drug-crazed psychopath wielding a carving knife had attempted to force him into a MAG to extort money.

As part of the original construction plans for the DELTEX HQ, Rogers had insisted on including a secure refuge within the research division equipped with its own long-term stores, communications and energy backup systems. It was a far-sighted and fortuitous decision. The two spent the worst period of the pandemic holed up in the refuge. Their connection with the outside world relied on social media and all contact was lost by the end of week two. Their only way of assessing how the pandemic was evolving was via their security surveillance cameras into the local streets. Eventually after six weeks had elapsed they were forced to emerge because their reserves were running low. What was awaiting them was post-apocalypse—a world in which nothing would ever be the same.

« »

Eight years passed. Rogers and Jefferson were still at Macquarie Park. From time to time they would visit a securely protected land holding near Richmond using a military grade ATGEV (All Terrain Ground Effects Vehicle) on loan to them by the Australian Defence Force and never reclaimed. Rogers had found a trustworthy family to manage the property. Their responsibilities included collecting rainwater, raising animals and growing fresh produce. Rogers left them with three quarters of all their farm produce in payment. But the main purpose of the arrangement was to set up a back-up repository for all DELTEX systems and data if it were ever in a position to continue production and development should the market improve.

It was a win-win arrangement all round, enabling Rogers and Jefferson to carry on at Macquarie Park, running a ghost enterprise indefinitely. Both would have really preferred to return to their home in the United States but could not ignore the likelihood that conditions would be even worse than Australia. The possibility of finding transport to get there was also remote. Rogers felt totally conflicted, his heart wanting to return, but his brain telling him there was little chance of his family still being alive. He did his best to bury family memories and fill his time working on his pet bionic Zapper project, without any particular reason since his former contacts in the US had all gone.

One day when Moses happened to be monitoring the surveillance screens, he saw a MAG had parked outside their main entrance. That was unusual enough, but the sight of a mixed delegation of rough looking men, one limping and middle aged, another similar looking 'bushy' and an elderly gent together with an attractive woman was enough to peak his interest and make him decide to find out what they were after.

CHAPTER 14 Macquarie Park – 2043

"This is private property!" The guard spoke unemotionally with a strong American twang. "What ya after?"

"We're looking for a 3D Printer," said Sam baldly, "that's what DELTEX do don't they?"

"No Shit?"

"No shit. I promise you!"

"It's what they used to do among other things—now's another matter. It's a very long time since I heard anyone round here asking about 3D Printers... You guys for real?"

"We're looking for a DELTEX 500 D printer to be precise—I believe that was the last model your company made immediately before the pandemic," Mayhew chimed in.

"And who might you be, Grandpaw?" inquired the guard rudely.

Mayhew was not to be put off. "I'm Professor Mayhew, a retired academic. I used to work in the University of NSW. My Faculty was possibly one of your best customers for that matter. A modicum of respect mightn't go amiss!" he said haughtily.

The man scratched his chin. "No shit!" he said again. "Got a *mod ic um* of ID?" He mimicked Mayhew, US style, making him sound like he belonged in the 19th Century. Sam was not expecting demands for proof of identity, but Mayhew surprised them again by digging into his trouser pocket, pulling out an old leather wallet and flourishing a well-worn business card with the UNSW logo on it. He thrust it under the man's nose.

"Holy Dooley!" He whistled softly to himself. "What do yer know! And what the fuck do you guys want with a 3D Printer? I thought the University would be out of business long before now?"

"You're right, it's long gone. It's not for the University. Mayhew here's just helping us," Sam said. "But we have a few questions of our own before we say anything more. For example, we're equally surprised to find that you're still in business here. How come you're still around? What are you doing?"

Moses took no notice of Sam. Instead he turned to make a call on his intercom. He talked softly for several minutes, looking back at them and their MAG, evidently describing what he saw, before finally resuming from where he'd left off.

"Okay you goin' to meet our Head of Operations here. 'Moses' by the way," he said, stretching out a massive paw. It proved surprisingly gentle as he grasped Sam's hand.

He escorted them into the building and up onto the top level via the escape stairs. Mayhew was huffing and puffing by the time they had ascended two levels. His face was pale and beaded with sweat. They stopped and waited for him to catch his breath. Serge was having his own problems with his prosthetic, but offered to help Mayhew up the remaining flights once he'd recovered.

"Can't leave you here by yourselves no way!" said Moses. "Sorry 'bout the stairs, there's only one more level to go. The elevator's not goin' 'cos we had to decommission the sucker. Was wasting far too much e-lek-tric'ty."

It was late at night, so it was difficult for the visitors to see what was going on in DELTEX, but there were many signs of cost saving measures and a skeleton operation at best. Lighting was down to a single line of ceiling spots following a straight path from entrance to access stairwell. The whole place smelt musty from poor ventilation and lack of air conditioning. It was badly affecting Mayhew. As he finally made it to the top, he continued wheezing and coughing his lungs out. "I suffer badly from asthma," he announced in a shaky voice, with no apologies to Moses, "particularly when there's mould. Extremely allergic to mould and there's a strong smell of mould and damp. Can't you smell it?"

Indeed the others could smell a dankness at the top level emanating from wall to wall plush pile carpet. It once might have signalled a touch of class, but now contributed to the impression of decay, with a visibly worn track from the head of the stairs to a single doorway that opened off the lobby. Moses rapped on the door before opening it, and gestured the others to follow him in. The room was very large with expansive picture windows facing south towards the Parramatta River in the near distance. There was a half-moon and they could dimly make out a vast plain of suburbia punctuated by tiny pin pricks of light, stretching to a dark shadow line of the Blue Mountains much further to the West. The room itself was almost dark, but for a pool of illumination provided by a croupier's lamp over a large uncluttered desk.

Rodney Jensen

"Difficult to get a clear view of the Blue Mountains now all those folks are burning fire wood!" drawled a voice from the shadows.

Sam's attention focused on a black silhouette reclining with his feet up on a chaise longue next to the table. He was holding a sheaf of papers up to the lamp, and had a pair of clear plastic framed spectacles perched on his forehead. He pulled them down over his eyes and seemed to focus on the newcomers with interest, before getting up and walking around his table. He looked like he was in his mid-40s, standing tall and thin with grizzly hair brushed back off his forehead. "I'm Hiram Rogers," he announced. There was stillness, a sense of melancholy and seriousness about him. Sam could not help feeling as if she was receiving an audience with a spiritual leader rather than a business executive. She introduced herself and the others in the party, as Mayhew found a bookcase to cling to, looking like he was about to collapse.

"Moses, fetch the man a drink!" Moses disappeared, before returning with a flask of water and some glasses, handing one to Mayhew who took it gratefully.

"Moses mentioned you're after one of our top line 3D printers," Rogers continued, in a voice that held notes of amusement and disbelief.

"That's right," said Sam. She gestured to the elderly man gasping for breath and sipping water. "Professor Mayhew used to work with one in the industrial design section at UNSW, so we brought him along as our consultant," she said, embroidering his status.

"It just so happens that you guys might be in luck, but I'm damn curious to know what you're intending to do with it and more to the point how?" He mused for a few seconds and then continued. "Although perhaps I can guess, but mebbe you'd care to enlighten us?"

Sam felt a rush of excitement at these words bordering on disbelief. *How could it be possible that DELTEX is still in business?* She had never met this man before, so she decided to stick to the most plausible reason why they wanted a printer, editing out the Aggressives and weapons programme for the time being. She pointed at Serge. "Our friend here, as you can see, recently has had an accident. It's left him in a lot of pain and difficult to get around without the crutch, as we're based on a country property. We thought maybe we could engineer a prosthetic replacement for him," she said.

"The hell you did!" exploded Rogers. "That all? You expect me to believe that. How much do you really know about DELTEX?"

Sam was taken aback, but not quelled. *What the hell is going on here?* "We'd never heard of this place before meeting our friend Mayhew over there. We've only known him for the last couple of days. Found him at the University of New South Wales where he's been holed up since the pandemic—probably like you? We discovered that he's been responsible for equipment acquisitions in his time, including your printers. He knew of its capability and of course we're interested. It's as simple as that. There's no hidden agenda," she lied.

"What she said to you is correct," croaked Mayhew from the corner. "I've never met these people before but I believe their story. What Ms … mmm, Sam has told you about me is entirely accurate. I have in the past been involved in negotiating with your company to equip our 3D Printing Division with the best technology available. Regrettably there is nothing left of the Printing Division or for that matter the entire University!" his voice tailed off sadly.

"Supposing, just supposing, I did believe all this. And yes, I can see the man needs a prosthetic. In fact we can make it for you no problem with the latest nerve interfaces, microprocessors, fully functional, you name it! In some circumstances, he could be walking normally again in say six months. But these ain't the right circumstances, as I'm sure must be blindingly obvious to anyone who hasn't just dropped in from outer space. How many orthopaedic surgeons do you happen to know who'd be capable of doing such an op., let alone the infrastructure to make it possible. In other words a state of the art theatre and a team of top surgeons experienced in bionics? A dime a dozen these days, wouldn't you say?" he concluded sarcastically.

"We do have access to some stuff ..." she started lamely. Rogers moved in one step closer, too close for Sam's comfort.

"I knew you weren't being straight with me!" he declared, eyeballing her. "Exactly what stuff and who do you have in mind?"

Sam realised she had underestimated Rogers. He'd seen right through her cover story. And she suspected that he had much to hide, himself. *Should I trust him? Where to start? I'm in a bind. But we need help. What the hell!* Against her better judgement she began.

"Hiram!" she cleared her throat and continued softly. "About a year ago, my husband and the organisation he worked for were wiped out by an alien force so destructive that it now threatens all human life on this planet!"

"What organisation might that be?" asked Rogers, cutting to the chase.

"One you've probably never heard of," said Sam. "It's an international US-based intelligence network with the acronym UFODD. It stands for Unidentified Flying Object Defense Directorate. UFODD's main business is to detect extra-terrestrial activity, and believe me there's been plenty in recent times. For the vast majority of people, it's gone unnoticed. And that's because UFODD makes sure the public never gets to learn about ET for obvious reasons."

"Not obvious to me, convenient for your story. But carry on. Maybe you'd care to enlighten me?"

"Public hysteria in a nutshell. For a combination of reasons including religion, no one on Earth wants to believe there might be superior intelligences out there. On the few occasions that the idea was put around that Earth had been invaded by Aliens, there was mass panic and disruption. I worked for UFODD myself and agree with the politics behind their formation. From my own investigations and what I have witnessed, I became convinced that the public were not ready for other intelligence. But now we're in a situation where it's almost too late to save the planet from total control by aliens. I've realised that the human population that's left now has to know about this alien invasion. We have to fight back before it's too late."

"What's your evidence for these incredible claims? I haven't heard of UFODD. And now you're saying it's been wiped out?"

"Yes the base in Central Australia where I was working, and all of its staff have been obliterated. I'm the only one left in Australia as far as I know, and possibly anywhere. I've had no contact with other parts of UFODD since we were attacked."

"And what makes you think I should believe this horse-shit!"

"I can prove it. I have plans of extra-terrestrial origin for weapons designed to combat the forces that have already destroyed UFODD. They can be fabricated on a 3D printer. I have the Apps to fabricate them with me."

Rogers looked gobsmacked and turned to Moses. "I'm mighty curious to know how this lady acquired such intel. Should we believe her?"

"That's your call, Chief," said Moses diplomatically. "Maybe if she produces the goods?"

"Wise words, Moses! You never cease to amaze me," said Rogers, turning to Sam. "Show us what you've got, maybe we'll begin to believe this!"

A shadow fell over Sam's face as she realised she'd talked herself into a trap. *Should I risk sharing key weapon designs with someone I have only just met? For all I know he could be working for the Aggressives. How is it that he and Moses have survived in relative comfort here for so long?*

She felt reluctant to voice her suspicions, but her expression betrayed her doubts.

"I guess if what you're telling me is true," said Rogers, "I can understand your reluctance to share your secrets. Although I still can't help feeling your story is phoney—or an elaborate con, which would be the real explanation why you don't want to be put in the position of showing me something you don't actually have!"

"It's not phoney!" said Sam flatly.

"Well how about this? We've got some plans here of our own. Been sitting on them since the pandemic. But now I reckon they might mesh neatly with yours— if yours are genuine. Do you think we should fill her in?" he asked, turning to Moses, who nodded slowly.

"I guess, to put it crudely, it's a case of you show me yours and I'll show you mine!" Rogers said with a smirk.

Sam thought for a few moments. "Would you mind if we talk about this by ourselves for a few minutes?" she asked Rogers.

"Why sure. Moses, find them a room can you?"

Moses guided them back into the corridor, unlocked another door that opened into a small room. It was bare of furniture but for a small table and chairs and was windowless. "As soon as you're ready we'll be waiting for you in Hiram's suite."

Once they were by themselves, Sam turned to Mayhew thinking that he was the wisest in the group. "What would you do?" she asked him.

Rodney Jensen

"I believe that what they're telling us is correct," said Mayhew. "I've scarcely had time to assimilate or even believe the story you've been telling us myself. Not that I have any cause to doubt you, of course. But surely, the situation is so dire, that if there is any chance of our surviving we must seize it. We're the ones who've come to them. You should remember that," he said.

"I think you've really stumbled on something here. You got to grasp it with both hands. I'm behind yer on this," said Serge. Gem nodded in agreement.

Sam stared at the wall for several moments before finally coming to a decision. "OK let's do it."

« »

Sam wasted no time in testing Rogers' offer once they'd re-assembled in his suite. "My team and I think that we must work together on this. You said that you have something to show us. We undertake to share our files with you, once you've outlined what exactly it is you've been working on and how it might help us," she said.

"OK, *deal*," he said. "What I'm about to show you has been under wraps a long time. It was commissioned by the US Defense Department, although that is something of a misnomer given that 'Zapper' is really about *offence* as much as it is about *defence*!"

"Zapper?" Sam interrupted.

"I'll get to Zapper in a moment," he said testily.

"Defense wanted something that would save lives on the battlefield, because public concern—no public outcry I should say, was hampering our campaigns, our tactics. Our men and women went into battle so covered in protective gear that they became easy marks for the snipers. Our casualties were increasing, not decreasing. And one thing the public did not like seeing were those rows of body bags coming off the planes into Washington." He paused to sip some water as he gathered his thoughts. Sam could barely contain her questions, certain she could see what Zapper was about. It was becoming obvious.

"You've probably guessed where this is heading!" said Rogers, reading her body language. "By the time we became involved with Defense, they'd had a lot of success with AI activated drones for surveillance and attack. There were also robots with specialised capabilities such as clearing mines and checking out enemy hidey-holes—stuff like that. What they wanted was a fully functioning bionic humanoid, one that could do anything a trooper could do—far more even, and expendable! The public wouldn't give a shit about the cost of a bionic. It was the body bags that troubled them the most," he repeated.

"The sad thing is that Defense never got to see the final prototype, nor anyone else for that matter. It was so heavily classified that very few of my staff even knew about the research we were doing, most of which was at Kingston U's AI lab in Virginia. That was before we set up DELTEX in this city. When I started this facility, I decided that all AI research was better off based here, for a variety of reasons including my liking for the country, its relative isolation, and as it turned out, your own defence people were also interested. But after the pandemic, I never heard another word from anyone else who'd been working on Zapper."

"Do you mean that you've been working on this entirely by yourself since the pandemic?" Sam sounded incredulous, but was growing more and more impressed by this unusual man.

"That's exactly what I mean! Yep there's been little else to do these last years but think and survive. But I don't want to raise your hopes too far. We're still a ways off achieving the vision we had in mind when we started—quite a ways still. Truth is, I simply don't know enough, although I've read pretty much all there is to read on AI. What I've realised finally is that the most advanced robots ever developed up until the pandemic were still sophisticated computers running on programs—damn sophisticated programs I grant you, some of which the computers devised themselves even, and no one in IT fully understood what was going on, but programs all the same. Pull the plug and you're left with a pile of non-thinking and useless junk. That's the truth!" Sam looked disappointed.

"I thought you were going to tell us you'd cracked 'Singularity'. I remember reading about it when I was an undergrad. There was real concern that once that point was reached there'd be no going back. Isn't that what all the theorists and prophets of doom were worrying about?"

Rogers nodded. "No singularity yet. Fact is, I'm doubting whether we'll ever get there now. All the best minds are gone or preoccupied with day-to-day living!"

Sam pondered whether she should reveal her extra-terrestrial information source, disappointed with what

DELTEX had so far developed. It was not even close to the technological advances she had observed at Alien City. But on the other hand, she felt that DELTEX would be the best option she would be likely to find, assuming Hiram would support re-tooling for something that he would not be able to understand.

"I guess it's my turn to show and tell," she said. "Can I ask you to suspend your disbelief and hear me out? The fact is that I've been in contact with an extra-terrestrial intelligence for some time. So I can confirm something that may not be what you want to hear—the singularity has been passed already. Not on Earth, but millions of years ago, somewhere else in the universe."

To her surprise, Rogers nodded with understanding. "I've had plenty of time to think about us, we humans I mean, how fragile this world is, and whether we're alone. Now that you're telling me we're not alone, it doesn't greatly surprise me that it's actually AI and not some form of alien life form on the other end of the line, knowing what I know."

Sam touched the pendant she habitually wore around her neck. "This may be the key to our survival," she said. "I'm told that the files on here will be capable of manufacturing weapons against the Aggressives."

"Aggressives?"

"Yes. Perhaps I should have mentioned that there's not just one, but at least two AI networks in the universe, and fortunately, we seem to be on the side of the good guys."

Rodney Jensen

"I'd be mighty interested to see what you've got on that pendant!" said Rogers.

Rogers took Sam and the others to a small console and monitor in another room. "The server is buried safely somewhere else. I'm not going to tell you where. It has a small nuclear energy pack that will last forever," he said casually. "Let me first show you where I'm up to with Zapper." Without having to enter any further commands the lighting went down leaving a three-dimensional figure standing before their eyes. The figure was dressed in military fatigues and certainly looked humanoid.

"Please explain to the folks here your main functions?" ordered Rogers like a showman.

"I operate via a database that in true-war situations is constantly updated with information on local terrain and disposition of hostile forces including missiles and drones." The hologram figure rattled off this information in an expressionless monotone. *They need to give him lessons in marketing and promotion*, Sam thought to herself.

"Currently I regret to say that the database has not been updated and is therefore of no assistance. In the absence of external support such as that, I must rely entirely on my own sensory capabilities, including x-ray vision as well as an ability to see into both the infrared and ultraviolet light frequencies. With my enhanced sensory abilities I can readily detect, for example, recent ground disturbance and land mines. I can see camouflaged artillery and hostile armament well beyond what would be visible to humans using special binoculars. I also have a range of weapons including lasers, missiles and grenades, sufficient to bring down a tank or conventional artillery..."

"Okay, that's enough" said Rogers, dismissing the programmed spiel. The hologram quickly faded and disappeared.

"To a limited extent," Rogers continued, "Zapper can function as a self-contained fighting unit in the battlefield by himself, relying on his own judgement. His judgement, I might add, has been one of the most intensively studied and contentious parts of his capability. Crucially it enables him to identify or distinguish between hostile and friendly forces with 99.9% reliability."

"Really?" said Sam, sounding disbelieving.

"Really!" said Rogers. "I'm not overstating his ability. But the reality is that public disquiet over a single innocent victim is not comforted by even this high level of confidence. We humans have a healthy mistrust of computers taking over our responsibilities. If you remember, self-driving cars had obtained virtually accident free capability nearly 15 years before the public was ready to accept them."

"I'd be very interested to see what my ET contacts have given me," said Sam. "Are there any readers available here?"

"Sure!" said Rogers. He pressed a button and the screen came up, listing recognised IT devices in the vicinity. On the list was a folder entitled 'Nest'.

"That's it!" said Sam excitedly.

She touched the screen and it opened to show a quantity of sub-folders including one which simply

Rodney Jensen

read *Open First*. It proved to contain a very long list of detailed instructions and manuals. On closer inspection, the amount of information and the promise it held was overwhelming. Apart from designs for a series of counter-weapons, there were plans for manufacturing robots able to undertake specific assembly tasks, and one capable of bionic surgery. "Wow that's one for Serge," Sam said.

Hiram leaned over her shoulder to take a closer look. She suddenly felt his proximity, a pleasing manly scent and warmth radiating from his body. She was briefly overcome by an intoxicating sense of arousal, and fought a strong desire to reach out and hug him tightly. Then she was suddenly brought back to earth as Mayhew, oblivious to her frisson of desire, remarked "I fancy you've got more than you've bargained for there." *Little does he know*, thought Sam.

« »

Sam and Rogers decided to go through the aliens' files together, while Serge, Gem, Moses and Mayhew were given the task of thinking up a strategy—and how to train themselves in the art of war.

The first meeting to discuss these broad objectives became quickly mired in uncertainty, once the enormity of the task was realised. "I've come to the conclusion that we can't do this by ourselves. We've got to establish a network of guerrilla cells, manage and arm them. Does anyone have suggestions how we should go about this?" Sam asked.

"Let me deal with the question of arms," said Rogers. "To my way of thinking that's the most difficult of the steps you've suggested. You see,

DELTEX has limited production capacity to churn out Zappers or whatever else your Nest have supplied us with in terms of their plans. And remember they're just plans. We don't know yet whether we have the capability or capacity to turn them into practicable working prototypes. They've still got to be manufactured and no doubt will need various materials as inputs. The ultimate goal would be mass-production of course, but I hate to remind you, all our Australian manufacturing economy has been trashed since the pandemic. There are no suppliers of the sort of things we're likely to need and that means we would have to become a completely integrated industry, sourcing the basic materials for the widgets and components we'll need—all by ourselves. It could take years to get to such a point, and judging by what you've told us Sam, time's not on our side."

There was silence for a few moments, as everyone realised Rogers knew what he was talking about.

"Have you completely lost contact with everyone in government and the private sector that might have been able to help us?" Sam asked finally.

"I wouldn't know where to start. The trail's cold. I've had no contacts with clients or colleagues here or in the US for nearly 10 years. You'd have to assume they're all gone—my family with them." Rogers face was grim as he said this. There was not much anyone could think of to say, as they were suddenly confronted by their own harsh experiences during the height of the pandemic.

Once more, Sam broke the silence. "I think we have to concentrate on finding the right people to help us, or at least do this in parallel with weapons development. Before I met Serge and Gem at their place in the Barrington Tops, I visited enough inland towns to realise that most by now will have been raided by the Aggressives. In any case, there's the logistical problem of managing them in remote locations and they don't seem a great prospect. I think our better bet is to concentrate on the main cities, and particularly this one."

"From what yer tellin' us," said Serge, "the only way we can go forward from 'ere is to start real small. We begin with one group, say football team size-like, work out what's needed and how they goin' to do it. There'll be plenty mistakes. We'll learn and build on 'em. Once we explained they're finished if they don't 'elp us, do they want to be captured and converted, that is, mebbe they'd join us. Yer DELTEX could work with 'em I reckon."

"It depends on which of the weapons we concentrate on fabricating and whether our 3D printing capacity is suitable for making it," said Rogers.

"That's a technical matter, surely? Let's first go a little further with Serge's idea of a football team," said Sam.

"That were just something I pulled out of me hat. It's nothing to do with football, it's just the size of the team I were meaning," said Serge.

Sam could hardly contain herself. "Maybe you've just hit on a model which *would* work. Of course I don't think there's much chance of finding football teams. People are far too busy struggling to survive. But groups of men and women the size of football teams, maybe gangs of looters, fighting over turf will be the way to go—people who are street-wise and have survived and want to go on surviving. They're the sort of people we need. The question is where do we start?"

"Round here's goin' to be far easier to manage innit?" said Serge.

"Pretty much an unknown—we've only just arrived. One of us will have to look around, maybe Moses has a better handle on this?" Sam said.

"Waal, sure there's different groups, mostly at each other's throats. Let's just say we don't exactly get along. Always trying to break in, breach our defences, steal our stuff. Get the picture? But it passes the time. They always come off worse—never learn!" said Moses with a wry smile.

"Perhaps we have to re-think this? Now we've got something to trade!" Sam replied.

"There's no chance they're going to listen to you unless we can get across what these Aggressives can do to them," said Rogers. "I think that for now we should concentrate on some of those alien weapons you've downloaded. You've experienced what Aggressives are like at first hand. What's your take? What should we look at first?"

"That's easy," said Sam. "I've witnessed the power of their self-guided swarms. As things stand, we're completely powerless to defend ourselves against them. It would be like trying to stop a fog," she said. "But we've come across a folder marked 'Nano-Particle, Cloud-dispersion' or something like that. When we read through the description of the device, it seemed to be exactly what we're talking about. The design is for a handheld weapon, which if it worked would be a game-changer. I think we should start with that."

Rogers nodded his head. "Yes that sounded like a threat nothing on earth could counter. But if Sam's right, the specs were within our ability to produce a prototype, I think. We'd be flying completely blind, but the only thing we can do is see whether we can source some of the materials it requires, and whether what comes out the other end works. Serge might be able to help us with his knowledge of mineral resources and particularly the rare earth ones."

Serge did not look happy. "Aven't a clue what yer talkin' about. But 'appy to look once someone can tell what I'm lookin fer."

"Maybe that data base Sam mentioned might be able to help us?" suggested Mayhew.

"We can all work together on this. The *Nano Particle Cloud-dispersion Device* is our first priority. Let's call it the NPCD prototype. The other priority is for Moses and Gem to start sniffing around for the 'football teams'. Is everyone with us on this?"

"Sounds like an excellent idea," said Rogers. There was no dissent.

PART 4
2044

Rodney Jensen

CHAPTER 15

As Rogers had predicted, making sense of the plans for the Nano Particle Cloud-dispersion Device, or NPCD, took up a huge amount of time. Serge proved invaluable in setting up a small kiln, salvaging microprocessors and batteries from waste dumps, negotiating with scavengers, and producing some of the esoteric materials specified in the plans. A number of input cartridges were needed for the 3D Printer, twice as many as originally designed. Rogers had to program it to pause at points in the assembly when a cartridge change-over was required. "If this works it will be a miracle," he muttered.

He and Serge could not resist watching the gradual particle by particle accretion model emerging in the neutral buoyancy tank. Its growth was imperceptible, *"worse than watchin' paint dry,"* Serge remarked. He was the first to realise they might as well be taking a break and it was well after midnight when he turned to Rogers, seemingly ashamed of his lack of staying power. "Reckon it's time to turn in innit? We can leave this runnin'?"

"Of course. I'm coming with you. At this rate we won't need to change any more cartridges until late morning. I only hope that there's nothing we've overlooked that might abort the whole process. It's sort of eerie having virtually no understanding of what it is we're making and how critical the various materials are, whether the ones we've sourced are pure enough. No point worrying about it is there? I need sleep too."

Rodney Jensen

They both left the laboratory, feeling reluctant to tear themselves away from something that seemed so important. "We could be making history here, you know," said Rogers.

"And no-one's 'll ever know, dead shame that!"

"I don't suppose there'll be a Nobel Prize any time soon, if that's what you're hinting at."

"What's that?" Serge had no idea what Rogers was talking about.

"Never mind," it was supposed to be a joke," he said lamely.

« »

Six hours later they were both back. "Couldn't sleep," confessed Serge.

"Me neither," said Rogers. "I can hardly believe we've got this far without a hiccup."

By now there was an identifiable shape appearing in the tank, with a cylindrical section approximately 50 mm in diameter smoothly transitioning to a smaller sized 'barrel' about half that width. The printer seemed to have speeded up and they could almost see the barrel growing longer as they watched its progress.

By mid-morning, the Printer light turned green, signalling the printing process was completed. The device now had a barrel about 300 mm long flaring out to a mouth the size of a trumpet. "Blimey! It looks like an old fashioned musket," said Serge.

"I guess it's designed to spray whatever it's spraying over as wide a field as possible."

Rogers donned a pair of heavy-duty gloves and carefully removed the prototype from the tank. He dabbed it dry with a scrap of cloth and set it on its bell mouth to drain.

"Mebbe time to get the others in; join in the fun like?" suggested Serge.

« »

There was an air of great excitement once Sam and the others in the team had assembled in the lab.

"That's it?" commented Gem dismissively, "doesn't look much, bit old fashioned ain't it?"

"If it does what it's supposed to do, who cares what it looks like. I think we're ready aren't we?" asked Sam.

Rogers nodded. "I'd like to quote from the manual about what we should be expecting to see. We haven't tested it ourselves yet, since we thought it's something we should be sharing. Anyway here's what it says. He picked up a tablet beside him and began reading.

The 'Nano Particle Cloud-dispersion Device' generates a wide angled particle field, which attaches to the particles found in the swarms and deconstructs them.

To test that the prototype is working correctly, the best results will be observed if it is set up within a confined space using smoke as a proxy for a swarm. The concentration of smoke should be sufficient to dim artificial illumination, but is not critical. Orientate the flanged opening away from the user. To activate the device, press the single button mounted above the handle, press the button again to de-activate it. Activate and de-activate for a period of no greater than 5 seconds. Correct operation will be verified if the smoke begins to clear immediately and within 10 seconds, is completely dissipated.

Rodney Jensen

Warning: It is not advisable to point and activate the device at humans, although we have engineered basic safety precautions to minimise deconstruction of human cells.

"That's comforting!" remarked Sam. "Should we test it here?"

"That was the plan," said Rogers.

"I reckon it'd be safer fer one of us to test this in separate rooms like, and we can watch on video," Serge.

"He's got a point," said Sam. "Anyone volunteering to be the one who presses the activate button?"

"I'll do it," said Rogers. "We can use the processing room next to this lab. It's wired for video. You can watch me go up in a puff of smoke!"

They set things up in the processing room, including opening the live feed to the main lab and switching off its smoke detectors. They put the device on a stand, so that once Rogers had completed the activate/deactivate sequence, he could back off and exit if anything went wrong. For his smoke source he'd positioned a waste paper basket, filled with crumpled sheets of paper, in the centre of the room. The sheets were doused in methylated spirits to help them burn more fiercely. Serge came up with a crude fuse to set it off—using 'basic bushcraft' as he called it. All it required was a heavy duty battery and a length of electric cable. One end was connected to the battery via a switch. At the other end, the bare wires were connected together via a scrap of very fine wire. Once the battery was switched on, the wire would instantly glow white hot igniting the paper. "Used it when we run out of detonators, always worked," he said, proud to champion a technology as far removed from the NPCD as could be imagined.

Finally Rogers and Sam were satisfied that the necessary steps and precautions had been taken. "We're ready to go," said Rogers.

There was a hush of expectancy as the team stationed in the main lab watched him put his thumb up to indicate *all systems go*. He switched on the battery, setting fire to the paper. The room began to fill with smoke. Rogers began coughing his lungs out.

"Shit forgot ter give him the gas mask!" shouted Serge. By this time, Rogers had already pressed the activate button on the device. He counted out aloud, "5, 4, 3, 2, 1," through his coughing, and then deactivated it. There was no sound apart from Roger's coughing, but immediately the smoke started dissipating. Within 10 seconds the room was clear of smoke. "Amazing, the air smells clean already," reported Rogers.

For a few seconds there was silence in the room as everyone absorbed what had happened. Then Serge started clapping, followed by the others, everyone jumping up and down, hugging and back-slapping Rogers as he returned to join them. Sam was the last to add her congratulatory hug. He held her shyly at first but Sam could not resist kissing him on his cheek and holding him tightly. Hiram looked deep into her eyes. He had an odd expression of elation quickly replaced by awkwardness. He let Sam go. She could not resist giggling, sensing that he desperately needed to unwind without an audience watching him.

Rodney Jensen

"I think this calls for a drink," said Rogers, conscious that the others were looking on expectantly. Moses vanished and returned a minute later with a precious bottle of bourbon and some ice. Sam proposed a toast to the success of DELTEX's work and found it difficult herself to remain cool. She felt certain that she and Hiram had crossed a line, but she knew equally that it would be preferable for him first to acknowledge his own feelings.

"I propose that the first thing we do is install this baby in all our vehicles," he said, an immediate convert to the Nest's weapon systems.

"I think we need to take a careful look at all the production files before we make such a decision," said Sam. "This is just the start, isn't it? At this stage we've no real idea what else there is in our box of tricks. Also, I suggest we start to think about your Zapper and whether there's a role for it to play in our defence strategy." Rogers' enthusiasm suddenly looked muted at the mention of his baby. Sam hadn't expected him to show such a lack of willingness to throw his own invention into the ring. It didn't augur well.

CHAPTER 16

Sam did not take long to set the wheels of production and recruitment in motion. Her first question to Rogers and Serge was how many of the NPCDs could be produced and how soon.

"From set up, our printer took 18 hours in round figures to give us one prototype. Realistically one printer could produce 5 or 6 each week at that rate," said Rogers."

"How many printers do we have in DELTEX?"

"Moses has already taken a look into our inventory. We have five printers remaining in stock and another five awaiting parts that we will probably not be able to source unless we can 3D print the parts ourselves. That would take quite a while for us to organise. Another possibility would be to cannibalise parts from the unserviceable printers. But unfortunately three of them have failed with the same defective part. That would mean we may be able to bring another two back into service, giving us a total of ummm … seven printers, and therefore a theoretical maximum production capacity of about 35-40 NPCDs per week."

Hiram paused to reflect a moment, realising that he had painted far too rosy a picture. "Sounds good, I suppose, but unfortunately, come to think about it, it's not that simple. We do not have enough of the specialised materials we need at the moment to produce anything like that number of printers. Serge has already scoured sources around here. To find more, we'll have to search much wider afield. We really need help on this."

Rodney Jensen

"How much of the input material, do we have right now?" asked Sam.

"Maybe enough for another 10 NPCDs at most."

"Okay, in that case we must redouble our efforts to recover more electronic salvage. Serge, can you and Moses think about how?"

"I've been thinking about it meself," said Serge. "I reckon we can kill two birds with one stone, in a manner of speaking. See, I'm assuming the scavengers we've come across might be able to 'elp us, join our teams, take pot shots at the Aggressives, yer know? They're like we been talking about. Survivors living 'and to mouth on their wits."

"Not sure where that takes us," said Sam uncertainly. "What would be their incentive to help us, and risk their lives taking on the Aggressives?"

"Simple. It's surviving they want. We can show them what they're up against, and we'll offer them weapons. Some may refuse, but others will help us. We got to try at any rate."

Sam turned to Moses. "Do you have any thoughts?"

"Sure do—several thoughts. The first is that we need to think up a way of systematically exploring our territory, preferably using aerial surveillance. We need to be looking for signs of Aggressives at mischief, places where there are concentrations of gangs, location of waste dumps, things like that. Maybe Hiram here has the smarts to automate it to a degree, come up with a list of places for us to visit perhaps?"

"I need to think about that. There's something at the back of my mind, but I need to check. It could be a real help if I can find the reference," Hiram responded.

"Anything that could help would be good," said Sam. "Meantime, Hiram can you think about some sort of mapping procedure for Serge and Moses to use to extend their search. We should set ourselves a goal of forming, say, ten new cells within the next four weeks and producing 50 new NPCDs to arm them. I think that should be achievable, do you all agree?"

"Before we go ahead with this, something that's been worryin' me," Serge said. "It's not just about givin' 'em the anti-swarm devices. But what's to stop some hothead turning one on us?"

"Maybe we need to build in some sort of programmable override if we discover anyone we give weapons to is using it wrongly," Sam said.

"I think Serge is on the money" said Rogers. "However, there's no way we could introduce such a modification without having a much fuller understanding of how the NPCDs work." He paused as another thought hit him. "Wait a bit! I've got a feeling there was a reference to this in the manual I saw. Let me see if I can find it."

He had already turned his attention to a folder on his tablet and was scrolling through it in search of a keyword. "Here it is!" he exclaimed. It comes under a sub-section entitled 'Security'. I'll read it to you:"

"Each NPCD will automatically be encoded with a unique serial number. The attached programme can be used on the Holo-Net to deactivate one or a batch of NPCDs by inputting the relevant serial numbers."

Rodney Jensen

"It looks like they've thought of everything," said Sam.

A week later the team were reviewing progress in terms of weapons production, and steps taken to implement Moses' suggestion of aerial surveillance using drones. Rogers was looking unusually smug, making Sam curious. "You've got something to share?" she asked.

"It was when you mentioned sourcing a plan for drones, I remembered discussing their use with the Australian Military. It was years ago, before the pandemic, and the main reason that DELTEX became established in Australia. Aus. Defence were very keen to be involved in our Zapper program, and joint research was actually sanctioned by US Defense. In our preliminary discussions, a key part of Zapper's operability was inputting terrain data. You might remember there was reference to that in the presentation I showed you."

"In order to test the viability of that concept, US Defense not only provided us with one of their state of the art drones, but also their production plans. That enabled us to modify Zapper's communication system so that a continuous stream of ground data was informing whatever mission it was on."

"You still have these plans! Why on earth didn't you mention this before?" Sam was struggling to keep her cool.

"I wanted to be sure before raising your hopes. The answer is 'yes', we still have the plans and one drone. But the reality is that your Nest systems look like they will make Zapper as relevant to our future warfare as a musket would to a modern blaster. As far as the drone's concerned, it's not in great shape after a collision with a high tension cable or something, can't remember the details. It needs a bit of work before it can become reliably operational again. We've tried making others from the plans we have, but we're running into similar problems of source materials as we've had with the NPCDs. Anyway, we have successfully produced one replacement so far.

Serge and I have been doing a few test runs and we can show you what we've come up with. Here's our new model," Rogers concluded with a flourish, removing the covering from a nondescript bundle which nobody had noticed was lying on a table at one side of the lab, to reveal a slick black-painted craft obviously designed for speed and invisibility in flight.

"As you can see," continued Rogers, "this drone is similar in size to a very large bird, but the resemblance ends there. Its specs are pretty fantastic. It can fly at supersonic speed while beaming telemetry back to base, including 3D video, sound and any other bits of the electromagnetic spectrum we're after. This drone can be programmed to track over particular regions, or fly in manual override, piloted by observers back at base."

"Wow!" said Sam. "No wonder you've been looking so pleased with yourself."

"Wait 'til we show you our video feed from the first two test flights," Rogers grinned back at her. He gave a sign to Moses who dimmed the lights and started the 3D footage.

Rodney Jensen

"In the first footage, you can see we've decided to take a closer look at what's going on in the centre of Sydney," said Rogers as the aerial view came up over the Parramatta River. They could see the wreckage of the once proud Sydney Harbour Bridge, and many seriously damaged and derelict commercial tower blocks on either side of the Harbour. The drone seemed to be flying low enough to identify people fishing, while unusually rigged sailing vessels, were tacking from one side of the Harbour to the other.

Mayhew observed drily, "I'm pretty sure those are passengers aboard. It looks like Sydney Harbour and the Parramatta River are providing a means of transport that used to be in vogue nearly 300 years ago."

Continuing further south along the spine of the City, they could see that Hyde Park had been taken over by squatters, leaving none of the original trees surviving. A pall of smoke hung over everything on the June day of the exploration. "Guess what they're using for firewood!" remarked Serge.

As they were watching, while the drone hovered over the Park, Gem suddenly noticed a warning signal and called out, "Telemetry! The drone's warning us there's another craft approaching. The telemetry on board the craft quickly pinpointed an image of the now familiar shape of a black 'Flying Container' on the screen.

"It's coming towards the drone," said Rogers, "and should soon be visible to the people below." They continued watching as it dropped out of the sky onto an area of Hyde Park that still contained the remnants of a large circular pool. Its rear door opened and a platoon of andronic guards jumped out. Most of their victims had already scattered, but the guards could be seen rounding up slow ones and herding them into the rear. It was all over in just a few minutes. The rear door closed, the craft ascended vertically to 500 metres and headed back the way it had come, quickly receding to a tiny dot on the horizon before vanishing from view.

"At this rate, assuming they are making regular raids like this, all the children, the elderly and the physically incapacitated will be gone," said Sam.

Nobody had anything to add. The sight of a once proud City Centre in ruins, with buildings in various stages of dereliction, the streets blocked with mountains of scrap materials, and the parks turned into large areas of mud, cluttered with temporary structures and denuded of trees for firewood, was hard enough to accept. But the human element was by far the most confronting. For the other observers in Sam's team it was the first time they'd seen the work of the 'flying container' at first hand in all its stark brutality.

"This footage should be our starting point for getting others involved in our campaign against the Aggressives," said Sam. "Show them this and they must surely realise that there is no choice. It's a simple case of fight or be abducted."

Rogers gave them a few moments to absorb what they had seen before announcing further news. "The drone works as we thought it would. We could see no reason why we shouldn't take a fresh look at Alien City."

Rodney Jensen

"You've already done this without consulting me?" said Sam. "Do you realise what you've done?"

For once Rogers sounded defensive. "We were acting on instructions to get this show on the road and get footage that will convince reluctant groupies to come on board. Wait 'til you take a look at this. It should convince even the really stupid ones. Anyway, for this surveillance we've flown over Alien City at high altitude.

As Sam watched the desert approaches to the prehistoric crater she'd explored some time earlier, it brought back painful memories. But she gasped when she realised that a shimmering dome of light now covered the entire formation. The dome rose to an immense height, registering more than 3,000 metres above ground level. It was only a few seconds before the drone's on-board sensors automatically took evasive action. It banked steeply and began flying in a circumferential course around the perimeter of what seemed to be a force field. The field was semi-transparent, enabling misty views inside the dome. They could see the shadows and spires of buildings occupying the entire land mass. The buildings appeared to be mostly high-rise and devoid of openings. There was very little unbuilt-on space to be seen, and what there was, lay heavily shrouded in shadow. Towards the centre of the site most of the towers rose close to the inner face of the force field. These were covered with strange projections with no obviously identifiable purpose other than possibly some form of alien communication systems.

Overall this new city looked like the work of megalomaniac designers. The beauty and natural ecology of the place had been obliterated to wholesale development and the creation of a completely artificial and controlled environment. The drone's on-board sound monitoring was picking up a continuous low-frequency hum.

By now, the drone had dived and was traversing the surface of the force field at low altitude and very high velocity, when suddenly one of the feeds showed a swelling on the surface of the hemisphere some three kilometres ahead. The swelling erupted into a tube. It was almost as if a volcano had begun to form with a pipe emerging from its crater. Moments later they could see a series of dots pouring from the pipe forming a globular swarm and then heading directly towards the drone itself. In a few moments the field of view was obscured. The drone had activated its anti-swarm device and the view became brighter for a few seconds, but then the feed stopped abruptly along with all the telemetry.

"It looks like we've just lost a drone. It's obvious it's been out-manoeuvred and out-gunned," groaned Sam. "I'd thought that at some point we might be able to make a repeat entrance into Alien City under cover of the natural landscape as it was, but that was fantasy. Look at what they've managed to build in such a short time. My first reaction is that we still need to build replacement drones, but there are questions now how vulnerable they'll be when the Agressives turn on them. I'm not happy about this Hiram. You've surely telegraphed our punches. Don't imagine the Aggressives will take this incursion lying down."

Rodney Jensen

"Why don't you look on the bright side," said Rogers. "We have a much clearer appreciation of what we're up against now. The drone we lost is a small price to pay for such intel. It's also saved us from facing the Aggressives in the flesh. We may not be able to tackle their main base, but we can at least start the second phase of your plan and intercept and destroy the Flying Containers."

Sam looked at Rogers intensely, as if she were drawing strength from his harsh impatience and thinking how to respond. "Maybe you're right, but it's a wake-up call that should make our objectives more realistic. We can only hope to carry on living in the cracks and tunnels outside their control of our civilisation, or what is left of it. Maybe we have time and numbers on our side. We can put the occasional spike in their machinery, but I'm coming to think we'll just slow them down a little, never overpower their main drive forward. If they can build an Alien City in so short a time, how long will it be before they cover our entire planet!"

CHAPTER 17

Serge's first serious encounter with a local gang was not encouraging. He had returned to base tight-lipped, wearing gashes on his arms and a livid bruise on one cheek. "Next time I'm taking a weapon, and I'll really make them bastards wish they'd never crossed me path," he muttered as he strode into the washroom.

It came at a time when Sam had still been at a loss to implement her strategy of finding groups of people willing to put their lives on the line. *How can we get them to believe the threat exists and be willing to offer themselves up against the immensely superior powers of the Aggressives. Maybe the footage from the drone surveillance flights is the game changer,* she had concluded.

Serge's barely contained fury immediately strengthened her original conviction about the value of his 'football teams'. "What happened?" she asked him, as he emerged from the washroom, mostly cleaned-up but wearing bits of cloth plastered to his wounds.

"A gang of six or so jumped us while we was fossicking among their rubbish and putting it in the trailer. Didn't matter that it was their throw-out stuff. They told us to 'fuck off', and we told 'em to 'mind their own fuckin' business.' If I'd 'ad me leg they might 've taken us serious like. There was only two of us, but we've got the experience and they'll probably think twice before trying it on again. We gave 'em bloody noses that's fer sure."

"And we've just been thinking about using people like them for our guerrilla forces!"

"Maybe, but not them bastards!"

Rodney Jensen

"Maybe you're wrong. They took you on didn't they—even with your missing leg you'd seem threatening. That took balls. For me it confirms the idea that a gang like that is exactly the type of force we need," said Sam. "Do you think that it'd be worth going back; try to meet their leader. You can bet there'll be one. People like that always have a 'Mr Big' pulling the strings. It'll be someone who's older, more ruthless and opportunist than them."

Serge shook his head doubtfully. "Not sure about that. Wouldn't want to put my life on the line with them creeps, let alone arm 'em with advanced weaponry. They're not trustworthy, let alone experienced and disciplined—nowhere near enough. The first real trouble, they'd break cover and run shit-scared I reckon."

"Maybe you're underestimating them. They've been annoying you because of the state they're in and their struggle to survive on nothing."

"Give me a break and don't tell me 'bout 'their state' or 'life's little troubles' ", he mimicked her angrily, taking her by surprise with his intensity.

She continued, undeterred. "No, think about it. They've lived on their wits all their lives and never had even a basic education. The ones you're seeing who've got the guts to take you on are the ones we need to help our resistance. Anyone who's less aggressive than that, is a lost cause. We need youths with testosterone and attitude. The more I think about it, the more I'm convinced it's the only way. I'll come with you tomorrow and we'll try to meet whoever's running things, and get him to cooperate. But we'll be properly armed this time."

« »

The next day, Sam, Serge and Gem arrived at exactly the same place as the confrontation had occurred and waited in their MAG. It wasn't long before Serge muttered, "here we go!" as a group of hoodlums came running up with rocks in their hands, waiting to lob them at their windscreen.

Serge got out of the cab ignoring the missiles sailing past his head and took aim with his sidearm at the nearest youth. "Put it down now or I'll give yer a lesson yer won't forget in a hurry." The youth ignored the warning with a sneer and lobbed another rock at Serge. He dodged it easily. "Last chance!" he warned as the youth readied his arm for another throw. Serge, finally lost patience and squeezed the trigger. The rock the youth was holding blew into fragments and splinters leaving the boy screaming in agony, clutching the bloody mess his throwing-hand had become.

"Anyone else like a try?" Serge said to the remaining youths in the group. "I might look an easy mark with me wooden leg. But the next one of yer's stupid enough to try your stunts again gets similar or worse. Could be a knee cap next time. Now you!" he bellowed at the boy still moaning with the damaged hand, "you stay here and me mate will see what he can do to repair the damage. Just think yourself lucky yer still alive. Meanwhile the rest of yer can take me to your boss."

The boys cowered as Serge waved his weapon at them. "Come and see what yer made of," he taunted.

"OK Gem you can stay 'here, see what you can do to fix his hand."

"I'd handcuff that idiot to the crash bar if I were you," said Sam. "Serge let's go, this should be interesting."

Serge had gained new fear and respect from the gang, having seen what his weapon could do. They started moving, but suddenly, one of them broke free and ran into a side path, ducking to avoid another shot. Serge pointed his weapon at the boy's retreating legs.

"Let him go," said Sam, "you can bet he's heading off to warn 'Mr Big'. We'd better be prepared for a reception committee." She pulled her own weapon out of its holster.

"Can't wait!" said Serge.

'Mr Big' turned out to be a gnarled old woman whose anger and staring eyes could have drilled holes through steel sheeting. "They tell's me you's causing us bother?" she snarled waving her own laser in their direction.

"We want to talk to you, but put the laser down now or you'll regret it," said Sam. The woman stared back for several seconds before her will to survive overcame her hatred and she dropped her arm.

"On the ground!" Sam insisted, and the hag finally let it drop.

"Watchah want then?" she snarled.

"Maybe we can help each other?" The woman spat out a large gob of saliva. It landed near Sam's feet, as she turned and began walking away.

"Wait," said Sam. You need to listen to this. Could save your life and everyone else's round here."

The woman paused in mid-stride, turned and walked slowly back towards Sam until her face was close enough to knock her over with the vapour of her rotting teeth and gums. "Now yer listen to me yer puddin' faced cunt. There's nuthin' I need from yer, not interested see. Just fuck off and leave us alone." With that she walked away and disappeared behind a wall.

"Went well!" remarked Serge.

Sam was not amused. "That woman's too stupid to bother with. Maybe these men might be more ready to listen when we show them what the Aggressives can do."

Serge nodded in agreement and activated a holo-presentation they'd made showing scenes of a swarm attacking a building, people running in terror and being sucked into one of the flying containers, an obviously alien craft, and vanishing over the horizon in a split second. The mocking and derision was gone, to be replaced with silence. "Those are scenes we've recorded recently," said Sam. "Not very far from here and the Aliens that are mopping up groups like you will soon be here. Now we have weapons to use against them, but we can't manage it all ourselves. Will you help us?"

"Wher 're the weapons?" asked the one nearest to Sam.

« »

The experience in gaining this group's trust and willingness to help, gave Sam renewed confidence to establish other cells of resistance on a more structured basis. She had explained her approach to Serge: "We have to set up groups at all points of the compass around Sydney, including the coast, otherwise the Aggressives will find a back door, and bypass any defence line."

During the next three months, she and Rogers began developing significant new additions to the weapons line-up sourced from their Nest files. They'd both concluded that what they had developed so far would be ineffective in resisting the Flying Containers or 'FCs' as they'd started calling them. The first new weapon described in the manual as 'Advanced Energy Beam' (AEB) could lock onto a moving target and destroy it. The second, intended to greatly enhance their defence strategy, was a remote sensing capability that could identify incoming FCs from distances up to 250km.

Sam had asked Rogers to work out a new strategy based on his demonstrated experience of masterminding a successful business. His first reaction was positive. "I can see where you're coming from with your 'all points of the compass' approach. There's no point whatsoever having a strong line of defence to the west if we're not guarding our eastern flank."

Rogers went much further, demonstrating his experience in management and planning. "History has demonstrated that fixed defences invariably fail. We've got to be more responsive and nimble than that. My starting point is for our cells to move within defined defensive cordons around Sydney, but they must be sufficiently mobile so as not to represent an easy static target. The outermost cordon would have, say, three main areas of operation, comprising Gosford, Lithgow, and Wollongong. Then there would be what I'll call 'the fall back ring' linking Palm Beach, Hornsby, Penrith, Liverpool, Cronulla and other centres in between. On that basis we'll need about a dozen mobile cells. They can be defended by the gangs which Serge, Gem and Moses are signing up. As an added incentive we'll be offering them state of the art technology. That should include the new NPCDs we've just tested, the interception device, the attack beam, and a new comms network."

As Rogers' initial thinking was refined, the plan became a series of peripheral bases linked to a central control node, also mobile, but temporarily placed in disused parking stations. The mobile bases were planned to move within their specified regions, and if under attack, could be supported by the nearest intermediate bases. The plan had obvious logic and was endorsed by everyone at the next progress meeting. Sam and Rogers were able to confirm that all the new devices had lived up to expectations and were ready for trial in actual battle conditions, but there was only limited progress being made in building up local resistance.

"So far we've contacted about twenty groups, and we've been negotiating with about half of them. The rest wouldn't have a bar of our plans, even when we showed the footage of what the FCs are doing."

"They might join us once they find themselves under an actual attack they are completely powerless to resist," said Sam.

Rodney Jensen

"That's possible, but many of them hinted that they were going to clear off to somewhere safer. We challenged them on that and told 'em that there's really nowhere that's safe. But they wouldn't believe us. The bastards still wanted us to give 'em our weapons. 'Fat chance' we told 'em," said Serge indignantly.

"Yes you did good," said Moses, "There are few enough of the weapons as it is and we're not about givin' them away if they're not wanting to help us."

"That's fer sure. But the bastards still weren't listenin' ".

"In that case, put them to one side and move on to the next group. By the sound of it if there are 10 possible groups we can use and we're almost ready to go. I suggest we start off immediately with the outer ring," said Rogers. "Are we agreed on that?" Everyone nodded.

The process of setting up the bases took several days, hampered by practical problems such as how to supply 10 new mobile bases with food rations apart from the high tech systems everyone had concentrated on. Taking another leaf out of history, Rogers suggested that they provide each cell with a written authorisation to billet themselves on any place that seemed able to house and feed them. "We'll draw up an official looking permit for them to wave in front of the home-owners. If there's reluctance to assist then they can find somewhere else. But you'd expect most households would cooperate when it's explained to them the risks we're all facing of being enslaved."

« »

There was a tense air of expectancy among the team once it was time to review the effectiveness of their latest counter measures against the Aggressives. Nobody was sure what to expect once a cell had been deployed and was actively resisting an overflying FC. Within the DELTEX HQ, a Command Room had been set up to monitor incoming FC Movements and communicate with all the cells. At the end of the first day's deployment, Sam and Serge met with Rogers to assess the damage. As usual, his report was to the point, un-tinged by emotion. "I can advise that during today's action our remote sensing picked up 10 FCs approaching the outer cordon. Within half an hour three of those were intercepted and destroyed. The remaining FCs changed course and headed south-west towards Victoria," he reported. "I can also report that the mobile teams now have a renewed appetite to keep on smashing these invaders. There is also talk of bringing in more of the waverers who now want to become part of this campaign."

"How long do you suppose we can expect the FC's to take this punishment without coming up with something else?" Sam pondered. "Have they simply diverted their attention to some other target, or can we expect them to react and retaliate differently?"

"My money's on them coming back with a few counter punches," said Serge. "They've got the numbers and the smarts. Realistically we can't beat that too much longer. I reckon they ain't going to stop with Sydney neither. Chances are they'll also be headin' in all other directions includin' Melbourne, Brisbane and Adelaide—who knows?"

Rodney Jensen

Rogers' report at the end of the third day provided confirmation of Serge's worst fears. "Today's news is not good. The Aggressives are showing every sign of not letting go of Sydney. We initially thought we had won a temporary pause, when no FC's were reported during day two, but late last night, 30 FC's were sighted heading directly for each of the interception stations. The stations responded with their attack beams, but this time the FC's were carrying new devices which reflected the beams back onto them. Within less than 20 minutes I regret to advise that each of the three outer ring stations and two of the inner ring stations were destroyed. Obviously this is tragic news for the friends and families of the victims. I'm not about to give up, but we have to re-think what we're doing. We simply can't continue sending our groups into an unwinnable battle."

Sam was shocked by the tone of his voice. She had never seen him this wounded and emotional before. But then she realised he might have been forced to re-live the tragedy of his own lost family. "We must withdraw the remaining inner ring stations immediately. Let's not engage any further incoming FC's, for the time, and advise all our stations of this," she said.

"Anticipating that this would be your response I have already conveyed those instructions. The remaining bases have been stood down pending your further orders," said Rogers.

"I'm glad we're on the same page with this," said Sam.

"Yer right there," said Serge. "I reckon the way we've set up our defence lines has been bleedin' obvious, too easy for 'em to get back at us." He paused, thinking what other options were left, knowing that Sam would be hoping he could come up with something more constructive.

"I reckon we're better off outing them almost random-like so we can hit FCs as they pass directly overhead. Give 'em no time to respond, then move on, whether or not they make contact. It's me *hit and run model*, not this defensive line thing. I remember me Dad tellin' me about that. They always end up getting' broken thro'. Didn't matter how much they'd been planned, or how strong they were. Always broke. Have to find somethin' else or we're about to lose all we've gained so far."

Rogers nodded. "I think Serge has a point. But maybe it's time to call it a day and start again first thing tomorrow. We've just got to outsmart them somehow," he said, taking the others with him, and tactfully leaving Sam alone to reflect.

CHAPTER 18

The attack on the DELTEX Headquarters came with very little warning. It was a warm summer morning, the first beams of the rising sun glancing on east-facing windows where Sam was sleeping. An insistent and jarring sound of a klaxen alarm jolted her awake, and acting in automatic mode, she got out of bed threw on a pair of jeans and top, before running down to find others assembled in the emergency area. She found a bleary-eyed Rogers helping Serge and Gem down into the escape bunker that lay below basement level.

Sam was feeling annoyed with herself that it had taken the unexpected attack by the FCs for her group to suddenly confront the vital importance of this refuge, including what it contained by way of provisions and the protocols that would need to be followed.

She could not help blaming Hiram for failing to mention anything more about it than its mere existence. Then she realised that she was being irrational, given their main focus had been on developing weapons for attacking the Aggressives rather than defending themselves in the worst case scenario.

"The FCs 'll be on us in minutes," Rogers explained. "They've been spotted approaching from Mudgee by the Lithgow and Penrith bases. Penrith reports they're heading our way, and Moses has confirmed that their approach vector points directly at us. Here he is," he said, as Moses joined them.

"There's only a matter of a minute or so left Boss. We can't wait any longer. Anyone missing?"

"Only Mayhew. I'll go find him. If we're not back in a minute close the hatch. We can't afford to risk anyone else," Rogers said.

Without waiting for Sam or any of the others to talk him out of his impulsiveness, he ran back up the stairs, pulling out his NPCD, ready to fight off a swarm.

Sam stood stunned for valuable seconds deciding what to do. "Moses, you go down, I'm going to close the hatch after you. Rogers, me and Mayhew are just going to have to take our chances."

"No way!" said Moses. "We cannot possibly risk our entire Command structure, simply because you think it's the right thing to do. I'll stay here, you go down!"

Sam, could not help inwardly laughing at the ridiculous stand-off which was putting them at risk against all logic and common sense. Fortunately, neither she nor Moses was forced to break the impasse in a way they'd have both regretted. Rogers reappeared, dragging Mayhew after him, both puffing with exertion, Mayhew looking completely bewildered.

Moses helped Mayhew clamber slowly down the steel stairs, while Serge guided his feet onto the rungs from below. Sam followed, leaving Rogers to secure the hatch. "Last in best dressed," he muttered as the sounds of explosions suddenly rang out above them. He followed the others down, pausing to swing the hatch back into position and rotate the heavy steel locking wheel. The sounds of attack from above were now muffled and their only light was provided by emergency panels mounted in the bunker's ceiling. With the six of them crowded into a space the size of a small living room, there was a subdued sense of defeat, no one knew where to look, avoiding each other's glances.

"Allow me to show you around," said Rogers. "Please pay close attention, because it's important you understand a couple of things. You may have noticed this bunker is actually a large reinforced concrete cylinder, designed to withstand, aerial bombardment. It's about 6 metres in diameter, and it's been built in this shape with enough strength to support the weight of tonnes of building material if DELTEX collapses. This area we're assembled in has bunk capacity for four persons. If my arithmetic is correct, this means that we'll be forced to hot bunk with two people at a time on watch on an 8 hour shift. I'll come back to the subject of watch-duties later."

"Beyond this sleeping and living space are three more areas including a space for surveillance and comms, a galley and storage bay, and finally a toilet and shower room. At the back of that area is another hatch that connects to an escape tunnel. That's been provided in case we cannot open the one we entered by, if say, it's been damaged or buried under debris. I had it excavated when this headquarters was originally built. It goes right under the main road beyond here about 2 km and ends up in a strip of bushland. The exit is located in what looks like a utility service building. It can only be opened from the inside and is far enough from here to escape notice from anybody who's within the complex and surrounds."

"Then why don't we use it now, for fucks sake?" asked Serge, throwing up his arms in a gesture of impatience and incomprehension.

"I don't think that would be a great idea," said Sam. "We need first to see what the swarm does and whether this is simply a short lived sortie."

"Are there any other questions?" asked Rogers.

"Watch duties?" Sam prompted him.

"Ah, yes. As I mentioned there's a surveillance bay in the next segment. We have video feed inside and outside DELTEX so that we can monitor what's happening around us. We can also stay connected with the bases we've set up around Sydney. It might be handy if we need help. The two of us who're on watch duty can take it in turns to monitor the video feeds and stay connected with our bases. Anything else I've forgotten?"

"How much food, water, air, emergency lighting time have we got now?" asked Serge.

Rogers was looking thoughtful. "I believe this facility was designed to house no more than four persons for two weeks. That right Moses?"

"That's right Boss. Even though we're 50% over what we were planning for, there's 10,000 litres of water in the tank and I've been regularly testing the water-recycler. So far as water goes with this small group (say) allowing up to 20 litres of water per day per person, could last for close to three months. The only thing is we all have to limit water for washing, including showers."

"And food?" persisted Serge.

"Should last longer than the water even," said Moses. "The only thing is it would get so boring you wouldn't want to eat!"

"What about transport? Our MAG's are in the basement. What happens if they're trashed," asked Serge again.

"Nice to see someone's on the ball," remarked Rogers. "That's also been taken care of too. There's a vehicle we kept on reserve parked in another building some distance from here. Moses has been checking it from time to time?" he said turning to Moses.

"Yes Sir! Regular. It's going fine if we need it."

"Good. I think we will."

"I have a question, and it's something we'll have to consider," said Sam.

"I think I can guess, where you're heading," said Rogers.

"If by any chance you have the means to do it, I think we must destroy everything above, including the printing system, the various devices we've been prototyping, the data storage and all the IT. Knowing you, I expect you've made provision for this?"

"Indeed I have," said Rogers. "This facility was designed at a time when a variety of possible risks were reviewed including conventional war, industrial espionage and of course—as actually happened—pandemic. I agree the time has come to pull the switch."

"I think you mentioned some time back that you had a data warehouse located elsewhere in case the DELTEX systems went down?" asked Mayhew.

"There's a hidden facility in Richmond which was established at the same time the construction of this centre was considered," Rogers replied. "All our data is backed up routinely. Nevertheless, it will not be a simple matter to start all over again. It will take us a long time to reconfigure another printer to produce weapons, for example."

"We need to know exactly where it is and how to access it," said Sam, "just in case we are separated and need to rendezvous there."

Rogers went to a drawer and found a box containing some small memory cubes. "These contain the information you'll need, but hopefully we can stay together if and when we have to vacate this refuge. Now I would advise you to put your hands over your ears while we activate the demolition charges." Rogers pointed at two red painted key-slots on either side of the drawer. "Sam, this is designed so that one person cannot do this alone." He handed her a key. "Insert your key into that slot and on the count of three turn clockwise I shall do the same at my end."

Sam did as instructed. "One, two, three," Rogers counted and they turned their keys, immediately covering their ears. There was a muffled roar and the building shook for seconds before the vibrations subsided and everything lay still.

CHAPTER 19

Without the benefit of natural light, the group lost their normal sense of time. The only connection with the outside world was the series of video feeds in the communications bay. The demolition charges had effectively created a pile of rubble above their main entry hatch. No feed of the interior of the former DELTEX building remained operational. But from surveillance cameras located well outside the complex, it seemed that the early-morning attack had been short-lived. No signs of Flying Containers, no swarms, nor andronics were visible in their field of view. But the all-pervading sense of their vulnerability, prompted Sam to express what they were all thinking. "They must have worked out we're here. Most likely they're just waiting to ambush us when we emerge. It's what any half intelligent attack force would do. Just starve us out, let time do the job for them."

The smallness of the refuge made the prospect of any extended stay unbearable. It had never been intended for more than Rogers and one or two other staff. The changing work shifts, with two of the six taking watch at eight hour intervals, was the only thing to break the monotony. Sam nevertheless, insisted that they should remain for several days before emerging. "It's a waiting game. The longer we can hold out, the less chance there is we'll find them still around, hoping to catch us out."

Three days went by, everyone realising they were locked in a life or death struggle, until Rogers finally got Sam by herself when it was their turn to be on watch together. She could see he was the most impatient of the team, unsuited to the tedium and inactivity forced upon them. While on watch he spent all his time carefully going over their outside feeds, staring fixedly for any signs of movement.

Sam could not resist putting her hands on his shoulder and starting to knead his taut muscles. He seemed startled at first, but quickly relaxed. He turned to face her, taking her in his arms tightly and began kissing her passionately. Sam felt a dam-burst of emotions inside her after so many months of suppression while in close proximity to Hiram. Her body responded to his loving caresses, she could feel her heart pounding, her breath catching. Then suddenly he pulled away, leaving her beached by his retreating tide.

"I'm so sorry," he cried his eyes moist with emotion. "I have really wanted this for some time, but it can't be now, this is not the place. I promise that I will hold this thought. You are the most wonderful person who has crossed my path in such a long time."

Sam simply nodded, swept with an unbearable longing to hold him again and shower him with kisses. Her thoughts turned to Byron whose terrible ending had long receded from her under the constant threat of the Aggressives and the necessity of dealing with the day to day by herself. *How long has it been since I have felt like this? Having Hiram so near but so far is making it unbearable. How much longer must I supress my feelings for him, enduring this interminable waiting in a cupboard! When shall we finally be able to get out of here and have a normal life again!*

"What are we going to do?" she asked him finally, with a great sense of let-down.

Rodney Jensen

"We've just got to get through this first," he said, staring meaningfully into her eyes. Then, continuing quietly, so as not to disturb the others in the next bay, he continued. "Over the last few days I've been checking for activity and there's nothing—zip! Strange I grant you, but there it is. Nobody else has seen anything either. What do you think we should do? We can't stay here forever. In my estimation, there's obviously some risk, but it's time to leave."

"You cannot underestimate the Aggressives," said Sam with her usual persistence bordering on stubbornness. "It's obvious they somehow got wind of our activities here—we were a precise target—they do not seem to have attacked any other buildings around here—they're all empty. Somehow they knew DELTEX was in business. I'm thinking that someone we supplied arms to has been captured and cracked or maybe they were able to read their thoughts. I suppose it had to happen. The chances are that they're still monitoring us—waiting for us to re-appear. And the problem for us is that the mere lack of physical evidence on the ground is virtually meaningless."

"Hoping to starve us out?"

"Blowing up all our data and systems will have made them doubly suspicious."

"I think it's time to use the escape route. They're less likely to know about that, and it emerges far enough from here for us to leave quietly, even if as you're suggesting, they still have this place under some form of surveillance."

"I'll bet my life on it," said Sam. "Their very calculated assault on DELTEX can have been no accident. I'm still thinking it's based on a leak—it's obvious. The question is: what do we do once whatever, it doesn't really matter—we've been blown we've taken the escape route? Where do we go next?"

"As far from here as possible," Rogers said without thinking, but then continued, "I'd suggest one obvious place where we can still monitor the situation in Sydney at first hand is Richmond. It's on the outskirts of Sydney and is located close to where we set up our reserve data and systems warehouse. We also know that its security has not been penetrated, assuming our surveillance intel's working as it should."

"Okay, I think what you're saying makes sense. We've got to re-group and start again. We can't give up."

"Let's talk to the others about the logistics at the end of this shift. But I think our feelings must stay with us alone for now?" Rogers suggested.

Sam looked him in the eyes for a few seconds, with an intensity born of love and sadness. Finally, she leant over and pecked him on the cheek. She said nothing more.

« »

No opposition was raised by the others to taking the escape route in the dead of night without delay. "Staying 'ere's just prolonging the agony," said Gem.

"Are we planning for one of us to take a look around DELTEX before we leave this area entirely?" Gem continued.

Sam, looked at Rogers before answering. He made no sign of what his feelings were. "I don't see much point. It's unlikely that there'll be anything for us to salvage. There's also the risk we'll be spotted if the site is still being watched."

"What about the printers, the weapons and things we've been producing?"

"Just going to have to start again," contributed Rogers. "We may have to get back some of the stuff we've issued to the cells. I'm assuming that we have some spare printers in the repository at Richmond, Moses?"

"Our records indicate there are two printers stored there," said Moses.

"That's a start. Maybe we'll find a way to 3D print a printer. It'd be a challenge, but we're not going to progress without them. Any other questions?" he asked.

"I am wondering where we can stay in Richmond? Is there anywhere near to the data warehouse?" asked Mayhew.

Rogers was looking doubtful. "Not sure," he said, "it's been a while since I was last at the place. From the outside it looks like a large fully enclosed barn. There's only one entrance door, and once you're inside there's nothing much but the banks of data storage and cooling equipment. It all runs off renewable energy. It was never intended for living in, simply to be identifiable as nothing other than an agricultural building to any casual passer-by, and very difficult to break in by anyone more curious. We might be better off finding a disused house to live in, or perhaps there's somewhere around the airport admin. buildings. But we can only check that out once we're there."

"Is there any security guard keeping an eye on that place?" asked Sam.

"There was a family looking after it, but they disappeared off the map some time ago and weren't replaced. Since then we've been reliant on security camera monitoring," said Rogers. There was a collective 'Uhhh' in the group.

"It's anyone's guess whether it's secure?" Serge remarked irritably.

"No reason to think that," replied Rogers defensively. "As I said, we do have extensive monitoring which as far as I know has shown nothing untoward."

"Moses?" asked Sam.

"I can confirm that the surveillance system is operating satisfactorily and there has been no evidence of break-in attempts," he replied.

"OK," said Sam. "Here's the thing. We've got very limited choices. We can't stay here because this location is well and truly blown. It will only be a matter of time before there's a return visit from the Aggressives. We just have to keep an open mind and confirm the security of our place in Richmond once we're there. The same applies to finding somewhere suitable to stay."

"The only way we're going to get to Richmond is in your spare MAG. Is it far from here? Can it take all of us?" Serge asked Rogers.

"I'll take you to it. It's only a couple of click's from where the tunnel ends. It can carry the six of us, but it'll be a squeeze."

Rodney Jensen

There wasn't much else to discuss. Sam brought the meeting to a close. "For Rogers and me who've been on watch since this morning, we need to get a bit of sleep before we head off. Moses and Mayhew, it's your shift isn't it? Carry on and make sure there's nothing else happening outside which might make us change our minds."

« »

They set off two hours after midnight. They had little to take with them except the clothes they were wearing and small packs of food and water bottles. The tunnel was dank and gloomy, lit only by low wattage emergency light panels. It was a short uneventful journey taking less than an hour to reach a small windowless lobby with a single steel exit door.

They switched off their flashlights and cautiously opened the door a crack, immediately feeling the relief of clean fresh air after days of breathing must and mould in their refuge. It was a moonless night and pitch dark. The area surrounding the entrance was a jungle of overhanging branches and foliage, underlain by weedy undergrowth and bush. Rogers, with the help of Moses, beat their way out of the tunnel and headed the few kilometres to where the MAG had been stored.

There were conflicting feelings in the group—of relief to at last be able to leave their confinement behind, but pent up fears about what lay ahead that kept them silent. It was not a particularly long walk, but seemed interminable, everyone on edge as they waited for the unknowable to reach out and bite them.

CHAPTER 20

In the wake of the DELTEX siege, Sam and the others set up a temporary base at the old Richmond Airforce Base, on the outskirts of Sydney. It was an area that had long ago lost its original purpose and had become a refuge for squatters not dissimilar to the UNSW Campus where Mayhew had been living.

The first thing they did was to fence off a large chunk of the air-strip and access tracks surrounding the administration buildings and hangars. It would have been a massive task at any time, but hugely complicated by the large population of refugees who'd moved in and taken possession of all these areas. There was constant obstruction, and the work was hampered by the people deliberately blocking roads, lobbing missiles and hurling abuse. Some were using their children to get in the way of the machinery and steal anything that was left unguarded. Neither Sam nor Hiram wanted to be held responsible for causing an unnecessary tragedy and tried to remain patient. But the buildings and air strip were resources they simply could not afford to waste. It took Serge with his peg leg demonstrating what his blaster could do, to keep the ringleaders at a safe distance. At night they kept the pilferers at bay with a pack of aggressive guard dogs on the loose and a network of surveillance cameras covering all the perimeters.

Using one of the DELTEX 3D Printers remaining in the remote repository, they set up a small assembly line to manufacture weapons, communication devices and armoured craft. Working in a second 'development unit' Rogers with the help of Serge reverse-engineered the last remaining printer and made various modifications to simplify the design. The main innovation was to enable its fabrication from separate 3D printed modules. It took them a month of periodic tinkering and refinement before they were able to produce a printer from the various sub-assemblies capable of matching the design specifications of the conventionally manufactured version. "Necessity's the mother of invention," crowed Rogers once he'd been able to verify this. "No stopping us now."

"I wouldn't bet on it!" remarked Serge, whose down to earth approach to everything wanted to de-bunk Rogers' hubris whenever possible.

Rogers also began implementing changes to their systems-backup, creating a new secure connection, potentially linking to separate data silos including one sited close to Bathurst and another for the longer term, in the Barrington Tops. "We've already seen one lot of data and equipment go up in smoke. Protecting our assets must be given the highest priority," he'd reminded Sam.

« »

Sam waited patiently to see whether Rogers was going to take their passing moment in the DELTEX Bunker any further, but she waited in vain. Instead, she decided to take the initiative once she could find the right opportunity to discuss her feelings with him in private. She wasn't sure at first whether he was simply avoiding her or so tied up in the day to day that he had decided to put the incident behind him.

In the end, she cornered him alone in the development unit while Serge was out looking for more scrap materials. As she walked into the lab, Rogers was busily examining a part that had just come out of the 3D printer. He was staring through a large lens magnifying glass so intently that when Sam softly whispered "Hi!" he jumped in shock. Sam couldn't help being amused at him in such an unguarded moment. "What's up Sherlock?"

"You startled me!"

"They say that's a sign of a guilty conscience, but I'll knock next time," she couldn't resist adding.

"Now I didn't mean that Sam, it was…"

"Joke Hiram! Don't take it to heart. I thought you'd be pleased to see me," she teased.

"Of course I'm pleased. You mean a lot to me, you should know that." Hiram seemed like he was trying too hard.

"Methinks he doth protest too much!" She couldn't resist plunging the knife in.

Rogers stopped completely what he'd been doing and stood up. He had a strange expression, like he'd been caught out, a naughty school boy look. He began again with an edge to his voice. "I'm sorry if I've seemed distant. You know it's difficult here. We've got no privacy. Everyone's watching us or maybe they're not, but whatever we do is going to be noticed."

"Who gives a shit what they notice or think? This is all about us isn't it?"

"Yes it is. It's a big thing for me you know. I lost Tina and the kids, and I just …" his voice tailed off again. He looked so forlorn and defensive that Sam couldn't help taking pity on him.

Rodney Jensen

"Hiram I understand and sympathise. I've lost my husband too remember. But he's gone and your wife has too. Are you set to go on grieving for her forever? Or is it something about me? Is that what's really bothering you?"

"No, no, no! Of course not. I … I have very strong feelings for you, it's just …"

"Just what Hiram? Can't you bring yourself to say it?"

"Sam, it's not about you. You're fantastic, strong, beautiful … Please trust me on this. Can we just put this on hold until I get my shit together? We're not kids. We've both got history. There's not a single day goes by that I don't think of my family and what must have happened to them. It's like having ghosts around me. God! Sam, I'm sorry." Rogers was sobbing, pathetic, diminished. Sam had never seen him so vulnerable and felt an overpowering desire to mother him out of his misery.

"Hiram, my love," she said, drawing him to her in an enveloping hug. "It's all right, it's all right. I understand how you feel. I miss Byron terribly too, but I can come to terms with it because I actually saw the evidence of his death. I know that he would want me to move on and accept that I could have feelings for another man," she said softly. "I can see you're not ready for us to have an intimate relationship. It's understandable given the circumstances. Maybe we both had a rush of blood at DELTEX and weren't thinking at the time, although I've felt no regret about what happened. And something did happen. There's chemistry, I know you felt it too, you can't pretend otherwise." Rogers nodded, responding to her hug, but not saying anything.

"So I can wait," she continued. "We've got all our lives ahead of us, even though they may be short ones if we don't deal with the Aggressives. But I'm going to say it. Hiram. I love you and I respect you. That's just how I feel, not complicated; don't care what anybody thinks; that's it. I can't make you love me I guess, but when you're ready to make up your mind, I'm sure you'll know. Meanwhile, I'm going to leave you in peace before I go and get even more upset myself." With that she quietly left the lab, leaving Rogers in his conflicted state.

« »

Meanwhile, the Richmond Base surveillance and monitoring activity had been kept in very low profile mode with minimum contact with the various cells which were taking out FCs randomly and unexpectedly when opportunities arose. It was a case of 'shoot and run', in what proved to be an exceptionally high risk strategy. Inevitably, the FCs had responded, by lifting their monitoring and surveillance capability and anticipating impending attacks more and more effectively.

By the end of the first month at Richmond, eight of the ten original cells had been destroyed and they had only managed to add a further four. It was obvious to everyone that the high rate of attrition was unsustainable and they had to come up with something radically different.

Sam decided to hold a council of war and bring matters to a head. She went through the grim statistics and then threw it open to the floor for suggestions. Serge was one of the first to put his hand up.

"Thinking around what's happening, I reckon we're not hitting 'em with the biggest punches we could. Firstly, there was Alien City. I know you tried to destroy it once Sam, and now look at it. And how do you suppose that happened?"

"Robots or andronics must have been the main way it got re-built so quickly I'd say," Rogers interposed.

"I think that's right," said Sam, "although the andronics would have to be key. That is why I think the Aggressives are mounting these raids all the time. They're probably working their andronics to death, literally, and they have to be replaced on a regular basis, otherwise their campaign would grind to a halt." She stopped herself abruptly, suddenly realising where the discussion was heading. "Serge, that's brilliant, we should have thought about this all along. We've been targeting the vehicles instead of the andronics, haven't we!"

"Exactly. It's where I'm coming from," Serge said.

"So how do we bring down the andronics?" queried Rogers.

"When I was in Alien City, I did find that they were as vulnerable to my laser as any normal human. I had the advantage every time because they were not well enough programmed to anticipate that sort of response," Sam said.

"Well I've got a very different plan which I reckon we should give a go," said Serge. "But the catch is we have to intercept and grab at least one of 'em FCs and know enough about how to drive it and communicate for the Aggressives to allow us to get into Alien City."

"That's a tall order," said Sam. "But assuming that I can get help on this from the Nest, and we can succeed in bringing down an FC with one of our Drones without completely destroying it, what's the rest of your plan?"

"It came to me when I thought that with our small numbers, there's never any possibility of matching their manpower, so to speak. We'd never keep up with 'em and their constant raids. Then I remembered a couple of things. First it were about them rabbit plagues in the bush—20th Century that happened, so me Dad told me—how the scientists found a way to kill most of 'em using some germ or other. And then much more recent were the pandemic, killed everyone nearly. So what I'm thinking is, suppose we could start a disease in Alien City, bad enough to wipe out 'em andronics. How'd we do that? Maybe they have enough human bits to get the same sicknesses we do. If I'm right, maybe we can wipe 'em out like the rabbits!"

"And what about us!" objected Rogers. "There are so many assumptions and problems with that idea. The most obvious is it would be incredibly dangerous for us, and could easily rebound on anyone who hasn't developed natural immunity to the pandemic, and that's possibly at least half of what's left of our population."

"There is a vaccine that UFODD developed. All staff were given it. But we'd need to synthesise tonnes to protect so many people and find a lab that could do it," said Sam.

Rodney Jensen

"What about the UFODD Base you mentioned?"

"I suppose it's a possibility, but a pretty remote one. Even if I could still get inside the place it's unlikely the vaccines would still be useable."

"What about the formulation, would that have been synthesised automatically? Something we could emulate perhaps?"

"Quite possibly, but unlikely that it was ever prepared there. I think it would have been brought in from the US, but I honestly don't know."

Serge was growing impatient. "Ok Sam. Yer and Hiram might be able to work out something there. Now let's say that we can turn our hand to producing them germs and a vaccine to prevent us getting sick. I now get back to the second part of me plan. We've taken over an FC and found some way of getting 'round the normal passes and flying requirements, whatever them Aggressives use to get into Alien City. Then what do we do once we're in?"

"Walking around and hoping we might act as carriers and somehow infect all the andronics we come across. Doesn't seem an exactly practical way does it?" replied Sam.

"I've been thinking mosquitoes. Mosquitoes like the ones which transmit Malaria, Dengue, Zika, Ebola-Z and PneuMox, them's just a few I heard of off the top of me head. We breed Mosquitoes in their millions, take them aboard the FC we caught and let 'em loose inside Alien City. What do yer reckon?"

"Holy Dooley," whistled Rogers.

"That's a brilliant idea, amazing even. Can you pull it off though?" wondered Mayhew.

"What was it you said Hiram? Something like 'necessity's the mother of invention,' weren't it? That's it innit?"

But Rogers was still deep in thought. "It's not quite as simple as that. I don't think it would be beyond the powers of the Aggressives to come up with some way of eradicating the mosquitoes, using a super-efficient insecticide for example. It's the way Malaria has traditionally been dealt with. No, what I'm thinking is something which would not so readily succumb to the obvious. If we could find a way of infecting their own swarms, for example, they would end up doing the job for us. Could be as simple as tweaking our anti-swarm device."

"I'll ask Leila," said Sam.

<< >>

Nobody in the group had disagreed with Serge's risky suggestion of attempting biological warfare against the Aggressives. The question they all began putting their minds to was the 'how', particularly finding sources of the original pandemic virus designated 'HRNX-0'. As Sam explained to the others, this deadly bio-agent had originally been developed by Australian scientists in a secret laboratory in central Sydney, but there was an accidental release that led to a pandemic, which had spiralled out of control, the legacy of the contagion still being felt decades later.

"UFODD developed an effective vaccine to protect all UFODD's workers. Subsequently the headquarters in Bourke contained a high-tech bio-lab on a separate isolated level for testing purposes, which only few researchers ever accessed," she said.

"It was top secret," she continued. "Because there simply weren't the resources to inoculate everyone, and if the public got wind of it, we'd have been under constant siege to hand it out. I still feel bad about it, having seen so many people dying horrible deaths, people who might otherwise have been saved if our industries hadn't been completely destroyed by that time."

"Where does that leave us now?" asked Rogers.

"I simply don't know. My husband Byron could have confirmed what was going on in the new base. He was employed there for several years after I was given my marching orders. I only got to find that out much later," she said bitterly. "As far as I know, there was also a bio-lab in a lower level which I never got to visit."

The mood of the room was sombre as everyone took in the many uncertainties relating to what had at first seemed a highly promising strategy. Rogers was the first to break the silence. "Looks like we'll have to check it out then doesn't it? But it's going to be risky even getting there and back from what you've told me."

"Yes I'm going to have to steel myself," said Sam. "It's got to be me for obvious reasons, I'm the best placed to find the way there and possibly the only one of us who might be able to get back inside the Base itself. Before you assume that I'm agreeing to you coming along Hiram, I'm definitely not!"

"See here …" Rogers started angrily, but Sam put up a hand to fend off his interruption.

"Hiram, no! Just listen. Whether you like it or not one of us has to stay here to keep things together. You still have knowledge of the systems we are using for weapons and countless other vital aspects of our campaign. We simply cannot afford to put both our lives in jeopardy with this virus strategy."

Rogers took a deep breath, trying hard to suppress his conflicted feelings of anger and protectiveness over Sam. "I guess I can support you on this, only because I understand your logic but I'm not happy with the idea of you going alone. You must have Serge with you. I really insist on that."

CHAPTER 21

While the team had greenlighted the bio-attack strategy, Sam knew that it would be impossible to proceed without help from the Nest, particularly information on the FCs. Even Rogers' idea of infecting the nano-particle swarms with HRNX-0 or some equally deadly bio-agent also had to be further developed. She prepared for her next Nest meeting by making notes of all the questions she intended to ask. She found a quiet space and entered 'LEILA_MN' on her Holo, the agreed passkey for contacting the Nest. She was instantly 'connected'.

We are impressed with your latest strategies, Leila said.

"Obviously you have already scanned me." Sam could not help feeling violated, her thoughts and intended questions already so easily intercepted.

We do not make a practice of doing this unless you call us, Leila replied smoothly. *We have reviewed both your requests and assessed them as feasible. The protocols the Aggressives use to enter and exit Alien City require passcodes you must enter onto the automatic pilot system of the FCs. We have sent you plans which explain this in more detail, including where the navigation systems are located and how you must pilot the craft in and out of Alien City, using the correct codes.*

The Aggressives will not realise we have taken over their craft?

We can't be certain of that. But the likelihood is that everything is programmed to work automatically once the correct procedures are followed. They should not have any cause to check your identity unless something unexpected happens. We are 99%

sure that the information we have sourced is reliable and you will not be intercepted and apprehended.

How did you come by this intelligence?

It is from what you would call a 'classified source', but I repeat we are confident it is reliable.

Leila paused for Sam to take in what she was saying before continuing. *Now if we might move on to the second part of your request, we have also considered the feasibility of modifying the Anti Swarm weapons which you have fabricated and tested. We would need to reconfigure them, so that the field they emit is adapted to intercepting and infecting the nano-particles in the swarms. We will therefore require the exact biological formulae of whatever contagion you decide on. I should mention that our Nest is already in possession of data for the HRNX-0 virus. If you discover information on other bio-agents, we can also adapt the weapon design accordingly.*

« »

Leila's advice confirmed Sam's thinking that a special trip back to the UFODD Base had to be made. She and Serge set off for the long journey into the outback, after equipping the MAG with all the spare parts and emergency supplies they could think of. Sam wanted to avoid taking the route she had followed previously (from her property near Bourke, ending up in the Barrington Tops). Instead, she and Serge agreed to take the most direct route possible via Lithgow and Dubbo, before entering the lonely desert region surrounding UFODD.

It was hard driving along what had once been the State's main arterial roads into the interior. Most surfaces had already deteriorated so much that in several places they had to turn back and detour. There was plenty of wild life to avoid along the road, but only in the town centres did they see signs of human activity. "We cannot stop and try to help anyone," Sam said when Serge started decelerating at the sight of a pathetic group of men, women and children, trying to stop them by standing in the middle of the road. "We've got enough risks ahead of us without getting involved here. I'm sorry Serge, but we've got to keep focused on the big picture." Serge nodded grimly and drove around the group before accelerating away.

It was late on the third day along the lonely stretch of track to the north west of Bourke when they passed the turn to Sam and Byron's property. Serge sensed that something was up and quietly turned to her. "Close to yer place? Want to take a look?"

"No, definitely not, please keep going," Serge could see her body language said otherwise, but let it go.

Shortly after that they discovered a convoy of burnt out military looking vehicles blocking their way. "This where your Byron …?" Serge wanted to know more, but was unsure how to put the question.

"Yes this is where Byron, Harcourt and the others were swarmed. They're buried just over there somewhere. I don't want to stop. Let's get out of here." Sam had crossed her arms over her breasts and was wiping a tear away as she stared fixedly at the road ahead.

"I've been dreading this, Serge" she confided at last. "It's just like I found them again, the only thing that's changed is the terrible smell has gone, thank God! And I'm also dreading going back into UFODD. It'll be like entering a mausoleum." Serge said nothing, but stretched out his arm and squeezed her shoulder. "Thanks Serge. You're my closest friend, and I know I'll always be able to trust you." Serge nodded, overcome by her intimacy, and the fact that she'd never opened up to him like this before.

They continued the rest of the way to the turning into UFODD Base in silence.

The only sign of human incursion along the entry track was a half-hearted attempt by someone to cut their way through the boundary fence and get around the gate. Once they had driven down the entry ramp, Sam found to her relief that her retinal scan activated the door entry, suggesting that Base systems were still working.

"I can't help feeling amazed the system hasn't been corrupted or somehow shut down after all this time. It's as though we'd never abandoned the place. It's just that faint odour, which is unusual. I immediately smelt it when we left the decontamination bays and the changing rooms," she said.

The ceiling lights came up as they passed along silent corridors. "I'd like to take a look around the whole building if possible, now we're here, particularly Harcourt's office. There may be information in her files, which were left behind in the rush to evacuate. You see, she kept some highly classified information from me which may have also involved Byron."

"You sure you want to do this? Maybe what's happened has happened and should stay that way. Unless you're sure there's some point in delving. I reckon nothing's to be gained by re-opening old wounds."

Rodney Jensen

Sam took a moment to ponder over Serge's wise words. "It's not so much the personal stuff I'm interested in now. More about who she was reporting to in the United States, including the last things that were exchanged before everything shut down on both sides of the Pacific."

"How about you do that and I'll investigate the rest of the building?"

"If you find a way into the bio-lab, don't attempt to go near it by yourself. We'll both need protective clothing and the isolated air supply connected before we go in. In any case the data is just as likely to be on Harcourt's system, although I may have to get Leila's help again to crack her passcodes."

« »

Sam and Serge spent a full two days searching through the complex before heading back to Richmond, arriving a further three days later. Rogers was impatient to know what they'd discovered, and whether it had been worth the effort. Sam got the impression that some of his impatience was a cover for his concern and relief at seeing her back safely. She could only hope that this would lead to a shift in their relationship.

"We had the usual problems along the way with some dills in Bourke and several other places trying to stop us and rob us like. But they backed off for the most part when they could see we were armed and not about to take any crap from 'em," said Serge.

"Fortunately we gained access to the base without any difficulty," Sam said. "I also discovered that I was cleared to enter the lab by my retinal pass. We found that there were cryogenic stores of various nasties, including HRNX-0, and most importantly, there was a good supply of the vaccine that was developed against it. There were other bio-agents that were being tested, but it seemed much too dangerous to bring them outside the lab and risk infecting ourselves or others."

"So where does this leave us?" asked Rogers.

"The main conclusions I came to is that we've got a viable lab there still, but the problem is that nobody in our team knows how to use it. We can't become bio-chemists overnight, and we will have to rely on the HRN-X0 samples for which there is a vaccine. Since the Nest have the ability to formulate HRNX-0 and the vaccine I think we should run with that for now."

"Did you learn anything more about UFODD and what has happened in the States?" Rogers continued.

"Yes I did. There was a chain of emails from the HQ in the Rocky Mountains which continued even after Harcourt and the others had evacuated the Base. I sent a reply message back to the last one received but there's been no response since I sent it—now five days ago. I'm afraid the trail's cold. And if a secure base deep under the Rocky's gone down, it doesn't bode well for anywhere else in the States, does it?"

"What about you Serge, do you have any thoughts?" asked Rogers.

"On the one 'and that base might be an easier place to protect than 'ere, but it's already been attacked by them Aggressives, and what's to stop them 'aving another go if they think we're up to summit." He paused for a moment before continuing. "So yes we might say it's sort of protected and lonely, but we also got to reckon on that making it too exposed to the next attack."

"Apart from the bio agent and vaccine samples, did you find anything else that might be useful?"

"Protective suits, a few tools we don't 'ave. They even had 3D printers, but I'd say nothing like as good as yer's ," he smiled warmly at Rogers.

"The one thing I spent most time checking out was the power plant. I'd guess it were based on them nuclear subs and it's probably why everything's still going so long after Sam got out of there."

"Could it be moved?"

"No way. It would need to be taken apart, but you wouldn't want to go near it would yer, unless yer happen to like glowing in the dark," Serge chuckled.

Rogers nodded and turned to some notes he'd been making. "One of the most important things to mention since we last met is the work we've been doing on the NPCDs as per the details the Nest provided. The other thing we've been doing is to breed some lab rats."

"I guess they weren't too difficult to find," commented Sam with a touch of sarcasm.

"Yeah, right, it didn't take too long to uncover a nest with the help of one of the local squatters. We were doing the family a favour as it turned out. Of course we couldn't just use any old rats, wouldn't be a proper trial. But they breed like … well rats and it hasn't taken long to have a couple of dozen semi-mature, disease-free ones. We've been waiting to test the NPCD until you came back with the virus and the vaccine samples."

"Good work, so what have you done with the rats? I've noticed whatever you've been up to has been under wraps," Sam was sounding intrigued.

"For very good reasons. We've been constantly reminding ourselves that we're playing with fire, and made sure we're all inoculated before exposing anyone to this particular bio-agent. Anyway we separated the rats into two groups. The control group has no protection, the others have been vaccinated. Both groups are housed in separate cages within a special enclosure. It's completely isolated from our air system, and has its own air supply and filters."

"To test whether the modified NPCDs were working we decided to use smoke again as a reasonable proxy for swarm particles. So we temporarily filled the enclosure with smoke and then fired a measured blast from the NPCD into the smoke cloud. Both the cages were open to the smoke filled atmosphere and we wanted to see whether it had become fatal to the rats which hadn't been vaccinated. It didn't take long for us to recognise that the ones that were un-protected were developing the classic symptoms of HRNX-0. By the end of day they were all dead. But the immunised ones are still alive and kicking."

"How much vaccine is left now after inoculating ourselves and 'em rats?" Serge wanted to know.

"We have about 50 vials left. For obvious reasons we must keep a very tight lid on these experiments. If it got out what we've been up to, we'd be under siege from everyone wanting to be immunised."

"And once we run out?"

Rodney Jensen

Sam had obviously spent time thinking about this. "We would have to make another trip back to UFODD and spend time figuring out how the drug is synthesised. We'd probably have to get a microbiologist on board, which seems pretty unlikely. I just hope we don't find ourselves in that situation, because in all honesty, it would be completely impracticable to even think about inoculating people around here, let alone the whole population of survivors around the country. That was also the conclusion UFODD came to after much deliberation, and the situation hasn't changed," she said.

"So where do we go next, and before the Aggressives turn their attention on us?" Moses asked.

"I think it's time to capture an FC. I've been looking at the details of how to fly them. It looks mostly automatic. All we have to do is enter the flight plan Leila sent me and we're in."

"That simple?" said Rogers critically. "This time, whoever is chosen to pilot the FC and attempt entering Camp-X, it cannot be you. We cannot afford to lose you Sam. We might as well give up otherwise."

Sam stared back at him without even a hint of agreement. "It's something we need to talk more about. Maybe we should be drawing straws, unless anyone has a better suggestion?"

There was silence in the room.

"Whoever gets the short straw will need to be fully briefed with the information I've received from Leila. Meanwhile, Moses, you're right of course. I think we must prepare for an attack on this base. The Aggressives found us at DELTEX and they'll find us here, it's just a matter of time. I think they probably underestimated our resolve to defend ourselves and that's to our advantage. It also may be the opportunity we are waiting for to capture an FC, assuming one of them lands and tries to round us up."

CHAPTER 22

Moses with his military experience proved to be the most useful player in fleshing out what he called the 'kick butts response'.

"They won't be expecting it, they're so used to us running scared," he said. "We have to be ready with our weapons. If they try to swarm us, that will be all to the good. There's the potential there to infect a swarm and turn the whole crew into carriers."

He turned to Rogers. "Boss do we have any idea of the gestation period of HRNX-0 for humans. You mentioned the rats started keeling over within the day?"

"That's right. My recollection from the pandemic is symptoms developed within as little as 24 hours and the victims mostly died within the next few hours after that."

"That's what I remember too," Sam agreed.

"Good. There'd be time enough for the FC to return to Alien City with a crew unaware they were infected. They'd be doing the job for us."

"That's all too neat. What happens if they **don't** try swarming us?" Sam asked.

"Then we go back to 'Plan A', overpower the andronics, either imprison or execute them before they have time to report back to base, take command of the FC and head for Alien City on automatic pilot."

All eyes turned expectantly on Sam to see whether she intended to support the plan.

"OK, here's what we've got to do," she said finally. "We temporarily reinstate our early-warning bases under orders, not, under any circumstances, engage with the enemy. Their role is simply to give us time to get into our positions if they sight any FCs heading our way. From now on it's vital the bases maintain watch 24/7, particularly at night when the Aggressives will assume we are at our most vulnerable. We also have to have someone monitoring our own comms at all times."

"Moses, I'd like you to refine your ideas a bit, and work out the best spots to concentrate our cover around here."

"Hiram, I'd like you to help me organise a meeting with the squatters. Serge, you'd better come along as well. I know we're not on exactly great terms with them, but if they understand this is a life and death struggle for everyone, we may get a few volunteers to help us man the defence positions."

« »

Warning of an impending attack was picked up by the Base three weeks later. It arrived in the early hours of the morning, when Gem happened to be the one on watch. It was sent from one of the mobile bases positioned half way between Lithgow and Bathurst to the west of the Great Dividing Range.

"Six FCs sighted, approaching on a vector of 125 degrees, estimated speed 500 km per hour. As per orders no attempt has been made to engage the enemy," Gem could hear obvious tension in the voice, which he guessed was from being forced to refrain from any offensive action against the hated FCs. Gem struggled for a moment to deal with the situation. He had been warned by Moses to maintain radio silence, whatever message was received, and his own procedures had also been clearly mapped out. He activated the warning claxon that alerted everyone on the base to the danger. He then turned to the wide-scan display and was able to recognise the closely spaced dots moving on a track directly towards them, from above Katoomba in the Blue Mountains. His final action was to switch on the PA system.

"Code RED! I repeat, Code RED! Everyone to Action Stations. FCs sighted, heading this way. Expect them to be over us in minutes."

No sooner had he got up to check the western sky than brilliant beams of light speared through the dawn gloom exposing the white profile of their buildings in harsh contrast against a dark background. The light sources were descending and Gem could now see the familiar outline of the sinister black painted FCs settling into the apron located between the hangars and the squatter settlement. He watched, as in almost perfect synchronisation, the rear doors of the six craft opened and squads of andronics, black pipe weapons at the ready, poured out. Three of the groups headed away from their building towards the squatter settlement, apparently intending to round up potential andronic conversions. The remaining three squads focussed their attention on their Base.

Without warning, return fire suddenly stopped the integrated assault in its tracks. Gem watched as several of the andronics fell in the soundless battle that ensued, while others, taken completely by surprise, seemed uncertain what to do, and rather than taking cover, started jogging back to their FCs.

Moses had arranged the defensive positions in a broad perimeter around the apron effectively surrounding the attack force and preventing them from escaping. It was a simple but highly effective strategy of containment and destruction. With the benefit of total surprise and highly effective arms, it was a case of 'shooting ducks on the pond' as Rogers observed later.

But what happened next was completely unforeseen. Rogers later swore that it had never been planned, as both he and Moses had suddenly erupted from their defensive position taking out any andronics left standing, and jumping aboard the nearest FC. The door slammed shut and moments later, the craft took off and headed back the way it had come at astonishing speed.

Sam witnessed what had happened and shouted to the other positions, "SECURE ALL FCs. DO NOT LET THEM GET AWAY!" But another one was already leaving as Sam was giving her order. "Shoot it down," she shouted again, and without warning it suddenly made an erratic turn and seemingly out of control spiralled down to earth, crashing into to the ground in an ear-splitting explosion and a searing ball of fire.

She hadn't noticed that Gem was just behind her, squatting on one knee, while sighting down the barrel of one of their shoulder-mounted AEB (Advanced Energy Beams). He was watching the four remaining craft waiting to see whether any of the others would be foolish enough to attempt a similar escape, but by that time they had all been secured, including numerous andronics, who were being lead out at gunpoint, their arms secured by plastic ties.

Inside the escaped craft Moses discovered that there were two andronics who'd been left on watch. One was at the controls. Moses, his laser weapon in stun setting, shot the andronic who was guarding the door, but both Moses and Rogers were thrown to the ground as the craft rose in an ear-popping climb before making a steeply banking turn and heading off at multiple G acceleration. For several seconds both of them were pinned to a bulkhead, but as the craft reached its peak velocity, they became free and were almost floating. Moses lifted the still unconscious guard into a seat and tethered him to the armrests. Then they both worked their way to the cockpit using the roof mounted grab rails.

The andronic pilot was seated at the controls, intent on the panel in front of him. Moses took careful aim, before alerting him to their presence. "If you want to live baby, don't lift a finger," he said.

The andronic simply ignored the warning, reaching for the keyboard, at which point Moses pulled the trigger on his laser. The andronic fell to the floor. Moses trussed him up, and with the help of Rogers, they carried him to the back of the FC, seating and securing him next to the other body. By this time the first andronic was slowly regaining consciousness and staring at his lifeless companion with an unreadable expression. "If you try any tricks it's all over. Period." said Moses, switching his weapon from stun to kill.

The andronic simply stared back at him without any emotion.

"I think it's best for me to stay here while you set the navigation protocols," he said to Rogers, who nodded his head and went forward again to take over the pilot seat. With his data tablet in one hand, he stared at the control panel trying to figure out how things were arranged. But it wasn't long before he slammed his fist against the console in frustration. "The Control Panel's modified from the one shown in the diagram. I'm really in the dark. I think we'd better bring one of those suckers back here and tell him what we want."

Rogers was taking note of the direction they were heading and trying to estimate how long it might take them to reach the part of Central Australia where he knew Alien City was sited. As he looked out of the cockpit screen, the view of the country thousands of metres below revealed a twisted network of rivers linking into one broader watercourse. It stretched as far as the eye could see both to the north and to the south.

"That must be the Darling," said Rogers, pointing at the endless band of brown water, "all rivers around here link into the Darling and end up in the Murray, to the south. There!" he exclaimed excitedly, "that might be Bourke below us," seeing what looked like a town with a neat grid of streets, about the size of a postage stamp in their field of view. It was located on the same side of the river as they were.

"If you're right I'd say we've got about 20 minutes before we're at Alien City, just enough time to set the controls, if we can make this *pile of shit* cooperate," said Moses, eyeing the reluctant andronic pilot, the one they'd dragged back into the cockpit, who was now conscious and watching them balefully.

"Listen, it's a simple choice. If you try communicating with your Base you're dead meat, if you understand what I am telling you, acknowledge what I have just said?"

After a pregnant pause, the andronic nodded.

"We know that andronics are capable of speech communication. Acknowledge my fucking order!" he shouted, his side-arm levelled at the andronic's head.

"I have understood your order," the andronic replied in a synthesised voice devoid of emotion.

"Good," said Moses more calmly.

CHAPTER 23

As the shimmering dome of Alien City appeared on the horizon, early morning light from the east glittered across the force field. Twinkling spots of illumination from within the dome, created an amazing sense of a vast and unearthly citadel, in stark contrast to the flat surrounding landscape of featureless scrub.

"Just remember what I told you," Moses warned the andronic pilot, "your job is simple: get us inside there and no tricks."

It was only a matter of seconds before the FC had closed the distance with the shimmering surface, now completely filling the vision screen. Adjusting the view with a control not unlike an every-day gaming toggle, Rogers was curious to see what lay below the surface of the dome. But as they were watching, spots of light suddenly defined a circular opening, revealing a brilliant background from the space within the dome.

"It looks like the force field has been neutralised to form a portal," remarked Rogers, as on cue, the FC slowed to an almost hovering drift and gradually descended. Both he and Moses had their weapons at the ready in case the andronic pilot was leading them into a trap. Moses could read Roger's shrugging of the shoulders, signalling an acknowledgment they were completely in the dark, and had virtually no way of telling whether or not the andronic was following their instructions.

As the FC transited from the air space outside the dome to the interior, the visibility changed in their viewing screen. "Wow, just take a look at that," said Moses pointing at the screen in fascination.

The space they were entering contained a forest of high towers, with projections at weird angles and cross-linkages at different levels that seemed to defy structural science and the force of gravity.

It was difficult to guess how high they were above ground level, but high enough for it to be uncertain whether moving dots below them were andronics, or some other life-form, and whether the larger elongated shapes, moving rapidly along a defined way, formed part of an alien transit system.

The ground area from their aerial perspective appeared primarily utilitarian with wide expanses of cleared platforms, an absence of green vegetation or any sort of humanising landscape features. But it was impossible to see very far in any other direction because the high rise towers blocked most of their view. From the few glimpses they could gain through the gaps, it seemed like the city stretched several kilometres.

"Look there's another FC!" exclaimed Rogers. "I think it must have come out of that huge slab shaped structure. And now I can just make out another one much closer to it. I think they're both heading in our direction. Makes me nervous," he said.

"Let's just assume we're simply using a similar flight path and that's where all the FCs terminate or originate."

" 'Grand Central', you mean! We're going to find out soon enough. Look! We're definitely heading towards it."

As they moved closer to the structure they could see it had a honeycomb form of giant hexagonal cells closely stacked on top of each other. The FC continued to descend and then changed course slightly so that one of the front sides of the honeycomb showing on their screen resolved into another portal, similar to the entrance to an aircraft hangar. There was a light flashing above the opening, and the FC, once again in its almost stationary approach mode, hovered and slid gradually into the hangar, where they could now clearly see andronic workers moving around.

"Uh-oh! Looks like we have a welcoming committee," Rogers muttered.

"It's just what we're after Boss, I'm only hoping our friend here hasn't been briefing them on the sly," said Moses. "Open the hatch," he ordered the andronic, who reached out to press a point on the control panel.

"We'd better cuff him to the pilot's seat," said Rogers. "We're going to need him again very soon. And I don't think we have much chance trying to get out of here by ourselves."

They left their pilot secured to his seat glowering at them, and made their way to the back to discover the rear door wide open. The other andronic was still where they'd left him, tethered to a back seat, preventing him from trying to escape or collaborating with the pilot.

"I'll go first Boss," said Moses as they hesitated at the door, sizing up what lay ahead. "Stay here and cover me, there's no point in both of us walking into a trap."

Rodney Jensen

Rogers, without thinking, refrained from arguing the toss, having come to depend on Moses' superior knowledge of close combat situations. He took up position with his NPCD at the ready, as Moses walked gingerly down the ramp and began heading towards the interior of the landing bay. It was only then that Rogers remembered that they had both forgotten to don their protective helmets and masks they'd been carrying in their packs. "Come back!" he shouted, but by this time Moses was already too far away to hear above a constant throbbing sound that filled the air once the rear door had opened. Rogers put his own on anyway.

Rogers watched in dismay as a squad of about a dozen andronics emerged from the shadows and surrounded Moses and the craft. Moses did what he could, downing those closest to him with an AEB (Advanced Energy Beam) so that bodies began to pile up. But he was already hit with glancing blows in the chest. Scrambling from behind the bodies he painfully made his way over to one side of the hanger while firing over his shoulder at his pursuers. He finally gained partial cover from a structural column supporting the roof, and held his ground, taking selective aim at those who were still in pursuit. By now most andronics were already lifeless, but Moses himself suddenly buckled under the impact of a fatal shot from one who'd approached him from his flank.

Rogers watching all this reacted without any thought for his own safety and charged down the ramp, firing his own AEB blindly at any andronic in his path. Only three of the andronics were left standing over Moses' body and he gunned them down without any restraint. Then he turned to his prone comrade.

Moses' face and body showed no sign of trauma but his eyes were wide open, his expression blank and at peace. Rogers checked his neck pulse but knew with certainty that he was gone. It was a realisation that put him into automatic mode, quickly calculating that he must somehow get the body into the back of the FC by whatever means possible. Moses was far too heavy to hoist over his shoulders so he resorted to the only other option he could think of, dragging his dead weight along the floor by the ankles.

He could never explain later how he had managed to accomplish this feat, including somehow getting him up the tail-ramp into the back of their FC. "I guess it was a case of super human rage taking over," he said with grim humour. "Of course, I knew I'd be stirring up a hornets' nest, and that was exactly what I wanted. It didn't take a minute for the Aggressives to direct one of their nano-swarms onto me. The cloud appeared the moment I'd got Moses into the back of the FC. I got my first real chance to test the modified NPCD. I sprayed and sprayed the swarm. It was a bit like aiming fly spray at a cloud of mosquitoes. It didn't bother me that I was playing with one of the deadliest biological agents known to man. Hell I'd been inoculated! Truth be it known I'd got completely beyond rational thinking at that point. Having dissipated the swarm I decided to do little more damage and damn near destroyed the whole of 'Grand Central' with my AEB. They kept swarming me and I kept pumping my fly spray at them."

"Eventually, sanity returned and I thought—*OK, I've done what I came here to do, now got to get out of this place.* I found my andronic pilot still cuffed to his seat.

Rodney Jensen

Remarkably, he hadn't managed to escape. By this time he understood the score. The moment I pointed my AEB in his face and ordered him to take me back to Richmond, he did what he was told. When we'd got as far as the dome's portal —Surprise Surprise, it refused to open. I ordered the andronic to pull back a couple of clicks from the dome's ceiling, turn the FC through 180 degrees and open the rear door again. He did as ordered, I aimed my AEB through the back door in the direction of the force field, and pressed 'activate'. There was an almighty explosion which rocked the FC like a cork at sea, and set some of the buildings in the vicinity swaying. But the shimmering dome was temporarily no more and we headed out with no more interference. So now we have two new andronic prisoners to deal with along with the others. The rest you know."

"We're well and truly blown. They'll be lining up their response team, whatever that is, hungry for revenge. What comes next?" pondered Sam aloud.

"I guess our immediate obligation is to Moses," Rogers said. "The trouble is I think he knew exactly what he was doing. It's going to take a while for me to come to terms with him taking the bullet; difficult to accept that he's gone, or to get around the fact that I should have tried harder to stop him going in boots and all."

Rogers paused a moment to collect his thoughts, angrily batting at the corner of his eye before continuing. "One thing we're not going to do, if I have anything to say about it, is turn and run. We keep hitting them when they least expect it. But first we need to check whether or not the AEB's done its work. We should be running a reconnaissance flight with a drone to see whether the force field's back, and if it isn't, then we mount a broader aerial attack on their city."

"Do you think it's wise to make another reconnaissance knowing what they are capable of?"

He turned to Sam, his eyes glistening, face rigid with anger. "Who knows what we can expect from the Aggressives? I guess they've got a few more unpleasant surprises up their sleeves, we've just got to stay on high alert and respond appropriately as needed."

He took a long breath, and walked off, kicking a stray mongrel out of his way.

Sam ran after him, concerned for his state of mind. She was not expecting to find him brusque and unapologetic for his actions, given what had happened. Her feelings were conflicted with an overwhelming sense of anger that he had done something so dangerous, possibly with the connivance of Moses, without consulting her. Yet she was relieved that he had returned back to base safely.

She found him by himself in his beloved work area. He was doodling absently on a graphic pad as though his thoughts were still locked away in his Alien City venture. He looked up in surprise as Sam burst through the door demanding his attention.

"How could you do that with Moses, leaving me in the dark like that? How do you think I felt, neither of you showing any thought for me or how I would feel Hiram? You just buggered off and I seriously thought you'd never make it back here. As it is …" she blubbered without finishing her sentence.

"You don't need to say it," Rogers retorted. "Yes, we sure fucked up, and I have to hold myself accountable for what happened to Moses. But you'll have to believe me on this. There was no conspiracy to leave you out of the loop. We both saw an opportunity and seized it, simple as that. After all, we'd had some prior discussion about this if you recall? It wasn't as if it came out of the blue. But the 'how' was never fully resolved, and your idea of 'drawing straws', I knew *that* was never going to work," he said bitterly.

"You know perfectly well if you'd told me what you and Moses were planning, I would have tried to stop you. Instead you went in without any preparation. Why for example, didn't you force the FC pilot to return here rather than allowing him to take you to Alien City, putting reliance on him for your navigation and safety? That was certainly never part of our plan, and you're very lucky to be alive."

"Look Sam, what's happened has happened. I'm sorry I've upset you. Now it's me that has to live with the consequences. I think we have to think about something else. I mean you and me." Sam stared at him with questioning eyes, but she didn't respond immediately.

"Our situation as I see it," he continued, "means I have to question your objectivity in opposing my actions. That's right isn't it? Do you think you would have been quite so angry had it been one of the others? You might have even congratulated them on their initiative! See, I feel just the same about you. I don't want to see you risking your life either."

Sam felt disarmed and mortified that he had so artfully struck a nerve she found hard to counter. "How can you or I put our personal feelings before the others? If you think about it, it simply isn't right. We are the leaders and we can't let our followers do all the dirty work. It just doesn't work that way."

"But if we can't trust each other, where does that leave us?" Rogers asked.

"We just have to agree to give each other the scope for independent thought and action, I suppose. I don't think it's appropriate for you to have to follow orders from me, and maybe you feel the same. In any case, it's less necessary than it might have been if we were a large group, we're so depleted as a fighting force, maybe we all have to act independently in a secure network." Sam knew she was babbling, trying to make sense of her emotions and the situation they were facing, but Rogers seemed unable to offer her any comfort.

"One thing I do agree with is we must make a return sortie into Alien City using a drone. Unfortunately we only had one and that's lost. It'll take some time to fabricate another. But it's a good idea and I will give it priority. As regards future planning and particularly risk sharing, can I suggest one of us at a time should take a lead in the future, surely we can agree on that? That is the logic behind the mission Moses and I chose to undertake," Rogers said.

"Yes, but at what cost! And next time, there'll be no more going off half-cocked," Sam responded angrily.

Rodney Jensen

Rogers simply laughed, making her even more frustrated at his refusal to take her concerns seriously. She stumped out of the room slamming the door after her.

« »

Sam, Rogers, and the rest of the group laid Moses' body to rest in a disused corner of the Richmond base. None held any strong religious beliefs, but Rogers, having been closest to Moses, took the opportunity to say a few words.

> *Moses as you know was a bicentennial born at the beginning of this Century from a poor background, went to war for the US Military in SE Asia in the '20s and came to DELTEX highly recommended after discharge from the Army which he served with distinction. On more than one occasion when he was working as my bodyguard, he saved my life including from someone who bailed me up with a knife demanding money for drugs. That particular arsehole had been watching our house in Newtown Connecticut and worked out that I always took the dog for a walk in the early morning. Until that episode I'd never realised Moses had put a tracking device and camera on the dog, and was keeping me under surveillance, even when he was supposedly off duty.*
>
> *Because of that and other initiatives of his, I offered him the post of Manager for Security for the new DELTEX facility in Australia and he has been with me ever since. He was invaluable in helping us survive during the pandemic period and looking after the place through various attempted breaches over the years.*
>
> *Since you all joined us and got to know him, you'd realise how much we depended on his wise counsel and readiness to take on whatever was thrown at him. As it's turned out, he*

was more than ready to give his life to put a spoke in the Aggressives' wheel, and we'll always remember him for his bravery when the chips were down. Maybe, some day, if we ever turn the corner in this campaign, we'll find a more suitable place for him to rest and be remembered.

Rogers turned solemnly in the direction of the grave, addressing his final words to his departed friend. *I'm sorry Moses; sorry to see you gone; sorry to miss your helping hand; sorry to miss your warmth and sense of humour. You've done so much for me and for all of us. How're we going to cope without you? You were like family to me and to all of us.*

Rogers solemnly threw a handful of earth over the wooden coffin, followed by the others, and was as close to weeping publicly as he had ever been since he'd been faced with the unbearable loss of his wife and children during the darkness of the pandemic years.

Serge limped over, wrapped his arm over Rogers' shoulder, and whispered in his ear. "Mate, think of it this way. He was a hero, no doubt about that, gave his life fer us, and knew the risks all along. We'll remember him, don't you worry. At least he had a quick end. I can think of many worse."

« »

The following week left everyone at the Richmond Base in suspense. Sam had kept her network of mobile watchers on full alert anticipating reprisals from the Aggressives at any time, but the skies remained empty.

Meanwhile Rogers kept himself busy implementing a new drone. "How's it coming along," Sam had asked him for the sixth time that day, only to be told "*Still processing*" before Rogers finally announced, "We're ready to start testing."

Inevitably, there were production glitches which had to be ironed out and it was a further week before the drone was ready for a return visit to Alien City, equipped with twin AEBs.

The atmosphere was tense in the Richmond command centre as everyone assembled to watch the now familiar terrain on the approach to Alien City. But there was a gasp when they realised, even from the distance, where the dome had been, something was now very different.

"Looks like they haven't restored their energy source yet," commented Rogers as the strange assemblage of alien buildings appeared without the intervening translucent barrier of the dome's force field.

Serge, who possessed the sharpest eyes in the group, had noticed something else. "Some of them buildings are smoking, and that's smoke not clouds," he said pointing at a deep bank of attenuated smoke, drifting high in the sky away from the complex. Moments later, the drone was over Alien City and sending a video feed of a totally broken place. Some structures had toppled and were lying in broken sections on top of each other. Dense smoke and flames were masking any activity at ground level. Most significantly, there was no aerial interception as the drone continued flying around and descending to deeper levels to confirm the extent of destruction.

"What do we make of this?" Sam finally asked Rogers.

"It's anyone's guess. But I'm thinking it cannot simply be HRN-X0 as we might be tempted to think. There were no effects quite like this when the virus hit Australia. Some utilities went down, sure, but nothing on this scale."

"It doesn't make sense, then, does it? Surely they can't have given up?"

"No, for my money it looks like a scorched earth decision by the Aggressives. Perhaps they found the place impossible to manage with too many sick and dying andronics and decided to leave it in a state that nobody could profit from. It's standard wartime strategy, but who knows how the Aggressives think. My recommendation is to bring our bird back here pronto in case there's something else we've overlooked."

"Yes bring back the drone, I need to talk to Leila," said Sam.

« »

Sam found her next communication with Leila cryptic at best.

"You are aware that Alien City seems abandoned?"

Yes we are.

"Why would they do that having invested so much effort in constructing their stronghold here? We assumed their plans were for the long term. How can our strategy of infecting their andronics with a lethal bio-agent have given us such a decisive victory?"

We are not entirely clear what their motives were and why they have now withdrawn from our sector of the universe. Of course they have accused us of our involvement because you have been so effective at putting a temporary hold on their plans. They have underestimated your people and we have also been impressed with the originality of your counter-attack.

"I am not convinced that it could be that simple!" Sam persisted. "Surely your Nest has played a role behind the scenes in all that has happened?"

You are an astute young woman, Leila responded after a long pause. Yes our intelligence suggests that the Aggressives have always chosen the line of least resistance. Your resistance to their invasion, given the primitive nature of your technology and systems, was doubtless not expected. More importantly, they have discovered another place where the inhabitants are likely to be far less troublesome to them than you have been.

"Where is this place and does it have a civilisation like ours they now intend to conquer?"

They are very different from you, at a stage of development comparable to your ape ancestors. They have primitive methods of communication but also have potential for conversion to andronics. They live on an 'exo-planet' many light years away from you. You will never meet them, and neither will any of your people in the next millennium. They are much too far away.

"Is that it? Are we free now? Will we need to call on you any longer?"

You should understand by now that our role is to guide rather than to participate, but we think the Aggressives will no longer pose any threat to your people. To us you are now like young adults who have reached an age when it is time to leave home. You must find your own way from now on. We have given you plans for basic devices which you are free to construct if you need them. However, our Nest forecasts that you will be facing greater challenges to confront in coming years, almost the equal of the impact that the Aggressives have had.

"What do you mean?"

There are many issues which your depopulation has temporarily put on hold. However, once you enter a new growth phase you will have to safeguard against your own impact on Earth, hopefully learning from the many mistakes you have made in the past.

To answer your final question, we do not intend to intervene any further. You must solve your own problems, unless you are confronted by another crisis, in which case we may or may not respond should you wish to contact us.

Leila promised to send software that would transfer control of the necklace devices that all andronics carried (similar to the one that Sam had carried on her first mission into Alien City). An information file on andronic care and maintenance was also promised.

« »

It took a while for Sam to forgive Rogers for his escapade into Alien City and decide how they might reconcile their joint management, confused by her own feelings about him. *Surely it's time for us to either cement our relationship or walk away from it, now that the future is more assured?* She mused.

Rogers had suggested the andronics they had captured represented huge potential to expand his production methods using 3D printing—if he could only show them how. One morning, she discovered him in the midst of a seminar attended by the andronics with Serge listening in.

Rodney Jensen

As she watched the presentation for a few minutes, a strange scene unfolded. The andronics were arranged in a circle of seats around Rogers, who with the benefit of an electronic white board was struggling to impart the complexity of 3D-printing procedures from inputting design plans to tailoring finished projects. But it was remarkably like he was talking to a series of sophisticated dummies. They sat in silence, not responding to any part of his presentation. All attempts he made to introduce jokes fell flat. Sometimes he would ask questions of his own, but none volunteered any answers. Finally, he noticed Sam at the door and announced that they would be taking a short break.

"I might as well be talking to the wall. They don't ask questions or interact in any way so I really have no idea how much they understand what I'm talking about, let's go and have coffee," he said to her.

"I don't understand why you are using this old fashioned method of teaching! They're andronics for God's sake. I'd be simply feeding them with electronic data which is what they're used to. But if you're set on this approach why not give them a practical test. Then you'll soon find out how much they're taking in."

"It's just an experiment. I need to work out how we might communicate. But I'm sure you didn't come here to talk to me about the andronics?"

"No it's far more important than that. It's about us and the future."

"Oh?" Rogers' body language was non-committal.

"The Aggressives have gone and everything's changed. We need a different game plan. How are we going to live in the future and build a sustainable existence for us and for others? And where do you and I fit in the future? Will it be you and me, or not? Should we go somewhere else by ourselves? The others have worked out that there is something between us and are waiting to see what we decide to do," Sam blurted out. "You need to let me know what you want to happen."

"Looks like you've been thinking a lot more about this than I have."

"That's the whole point! So far it seems like you have carefully avoided these questions and any form of commitment. You seem stuck in the past as far as relationships are concerned, which makes me feel pretty uncomfortable. Whether you like it or not, we crossed a line back there in DELTEX."

Rogers nodded uncertainly, "I guess we did."

"For me there is no going back. But for you it seems like retreat is what you're after. Please tell me if I'm wrong. Because I have to know—there's either a future for me with you or there isn't. If there isn't, I must move on, we're too closely connected in our present space and I'm tired of pretending we're just good friends or fellow workers. I want more. We can't go on like this."

"Sounds like an ultimatum," Rogers seemed fidgety and uncertain what to say.

"Look Hiram, I can't force you to feel the way I do, and I came prepared for you to offer me a non-answer like that. So I've decided it's time to go our separate ways. I want to go back to the Barrington Tops. I'll take half the andronics, and Serge, Gem and Mayhew can join me if they want to. You can do what you like.

Richmond's yours as far as I'm concerned. You may also want to consider finding a role for some of the personnel who took part in our defences."

"I'm sorry it's come to this."

"So am I," said Sam wearily.

PART 5
Re-Settlement
- 2049

Rodney Jensen

CHAPTER 24

The first day back in the Barrington Tops was dispiriting. Each one of the team who'd lived there before held good memories of the place, with high hopes for the future. But the moment they had reached the final entry track, deeply rutted and eroded by rain, with no signs of any attempted maintenance, their optimism was dashed.

As they entered the former settlement, it appeared almost derelict, with only a few villagers left who seemed to be struggling and subsisting on what they could grow or forage. There were no younger people or children to be seen. Beyond the cheerless atmosphere of the shacks, those that were still standing that is, young native eucalypts and acacia saplings were appearing, threatening to take over what had once been flourishing vegetable gardens. An abundance of fresh animal droppings also showed the inevitable return of the wildlife once the people had left.

Serge, the original founder of the Barrington Tops community, was even more overcome when he discovered the kiln and foundry, its former lifeblood now completely abandoned.

"And as fer this place—what can yer say?" he remarked, as he cast his eyes around the abandoned brickwork of the kiln, the ground merely left with rain soaked runnels of carbon ash and the hearth, cold and moss-covered. "It's a pretty sorry mess, no doubt about that. But we'll fire things up again, yer can count on it."

Rodney Jensen

"I'm wondering what went wrong here?" Mayhew muttered to Sam in an aside. "You gave me the distinct impression that this place was a going concern. I suppose that there's nothing left for the people without the foundry, is there?"

She could hardly disagree with him, and was surprised as much as the others. "No that's right. It looks like when Serge, Gem and I decided to head off for Sydney, we left the others without the will to keep things going. So now we have to decide whether it's worth starting all over again. But at least we don't have to worry about the Aggressives, if Leila's to be believed."

Serge joined in the conversation. "I reckon we can turn the foundry over to our andronics now. Start afresh like. Looking at what's left of the old foundry, it's all fit fer the junk heap anyway!"

"You've got a point—but what's the new plan?" Sam asked.

"Get Rogers involved. Mebbe 'e'll help us re-plan the whole thing—show us what to do like. And mebbe there's easier ways than crushin' 'n meltin' ore and pourin' it into moulds. I've seen what he can do with 'em printers. If we can use some of 'em new materials and 3D print instead … come to think of it, we don't really need to make metal tools and stuff, we can make just about anything with synthetics and much simpler."

"You'll have to ask Rogers about that yourself! You could even go into partnership with him, if you want," said Sam bitterly. Serge backed away realising how sensitive Sam was about him.

Serge's enthusiasm to bring different production methods to the settlement, with the remote assistance of Rogers, inevitably changed the direction of the place they'd decided to name 'Prospect' rather than 'the Foundry'. It gave Serge a new purpose and opportunity to develop better ways of producing and selling their products locally. He realised they needed to find a place to sell their wares more publicly, instead of waiting for people to come trudging up the hill looking for the odd axe-head or hammer, as they had in the past.

Rogers also made him see an equally fundamental constraint on his manufacturing ambitions. It happened as a throwaway line while Serge was updating him on how things were going while talking over their secure network. "I think one of the biggest obstacles we face in picking up the pieces after the pandemic and the Aggressives—it's not just the lack of demand for anything we manufacture, but the means of exchange," Rogers said.

"Yer've lost me there," said Serge.

"Most places you come across have to barter because there's no longer any money to buy things, no banks to save it in, the whole financial structure's gone and without it we're all marooned in a past when you had to swap a horse shoe for a piglet, even if you didn't really want the piglet."

"Yer right there," said Serge ruefully, reflecting on their own store at Prospect which by degrees was filling up with a range of items he'd reluctantly accepted in order to complete a deal. For him, that discussion led to a light bulb moment and triggered an

Rodney Jensen

entirely new venture. Before long Rogers had helped Serge re-tool his product range with the help of their andronics. They also worked on a simple APP that enabled a standard holo to act as a card reader, which combined with credit cards, could provide their potential customers with a new means of purchasing things.

« »

Daisy Schmidt wiped her brow with a scrap of cloth hanging from her pinafore. There was a cloudless sky and the temperatures outside were routinely in the high '40s. *At least it's dry heat*, she reflected, even so her broad hat and loose fitting clothes were obligatory.

She'd been standing at the counter since early morning and her customers had been sporadic, preferring to spend time chatting rather than actually buying her groceries and hardware. A middle aged man entered her shop, carrying a large leather pouch, and walking with a rolling gait. He carefully closed the door and approached the counter. He had a rustic look about him, but his gaze was intense as he pulled off his bush hat and mopped his sweating brow with a large bandana.

"What can I do fer yer?" Daisy asked him brightly.

"I'm new to these parts, but I saw yer general store, and thought yer'd be interested in some of the things we're selling."

"Pretty well covered by our usual suppliers, as it happens, but let's take a look at what yer have."

"This 'ere's some of our product range," he said opening his pouch and pulling out a large tablet device.

"Now what you got there? Ain't seen one of them for a long time," Dolly breathed in amazement. Serge touched the side and a three dimensional image of a bushland setting appeared on its desktop. A series of icons appeared in various parts of the scene with names such as 'Farm', 'Home', 'Gardening', 'Hunting', 'Fishing', 'Toys and Hobbies'. That last one there's not got anything in it yet," said Serge apologetically pointing at the 'Toys and Hobbies' icon. "There's a lot more to come, but any of the other ranges you'd like to see in particular?"

"Please can I hold it?" asked Daisy excitedly. Serge let her take it from him.

"Now let me see …" She cradled the tablet in her arms as gently as though it were a baby, touching its rounded edges and crystal clear display in total amazement. Then she gently moved her finger towards the 'Home' icon and the screen immediately displayed pages of a catalogue, with images of pots and pans, containers, simple essentials like brushes and mops.

"So where yer from," she asked, giving herself time to take it all in.

"Barrington Tops way," he said vaguely, "quite some distance from here. But we're planning regular visits to all our wholesale customers in the future."

"Hmm. Like the look of these things," she said finally, after carefully examining every item in the Home catalogue. "How would you want to be paid? In-kind, like?"

"Well it's like this, Missus," he began formally.

"Just call me 'Daisy'," she interrupted.

Rodney Jensen

"We're starting this new way of paying fer things soon. We think it will suit everyone better than having to exchange stuff. But until we get this off the ground, we'll take whatever yer have to offer in payment at an agreed rate of credit."

The woman was looking confused. "Oh, I'm not sure. Our deals are always set at the time we buy or sell something, and as yer'd understand, I'm sure, it depends how much the things are worth to our customers at that time. There's no fixed rates on anything we exchange."

"We understand, Daisy. But this 'ere's a new system. We'll give yer a merchant card and a special reader guaranteed secure. You'll soon realise the advantage of using our credit system rather than bargaining. To get yer goin' we're ready to accept deposits in the form of merchandise, whatever yer want. We've drawn up a basic value chart for nearly anythin' yer might 'ave in stock. And we'll give yer a copy to help yer fix yer price fer all yer customers. It's different from what yer used to but once yer get it up and runnin' yer'll never look back!"

"Well yer sound like yer know what yer doin'," Daisy said uncertainly, "but most 'round 'ere 'll be thinkin' we learnt our lesson with them banks—never trust the buggers! See particuly the older ones remember losin' all their savin's years back. Take a long time for us to ever trust a bank again. Why would we? What guarantees can yer give us?"

Serge paused to reflect on the question he knew he'd be getting. "So long as we're around we'll guarantee that yer credit's covered. For those willing to sign up, we're willing to produce a summary of our structure like. The more sign up, the stronger it will become."

The conversation continued longer than Serge was expecting. Daisy turned out to be very shrewd in all matters financial and quickly realised that she might be in a position to embrace the system and share in its potential. The clincher was when Serge painted a broader picture of gains that could be made by the community.

"Well, here's another thought for yer," Serge said "The reason we're offering this is not for our own benefit, so much as a way to lift businesses 'round here out of the trough they've fallen into. At the moment, goods have no standard values and their worth depends on the bargaining skills of who sells or buys the stuff. Our new way of doing things saves yer from being cheated by low-lifes, and there's plenty of them around." Daisy nodded signalling she knew from experience exactly where he was coming from.

"Everyone stands to benefit when goods are bought and sold at more standard rates and it's more convenient than bargaining because it takes away the need for either side to have something they actually want to trade. I'm sure that yer've found that your customers are often like that or what they want to offer for trading purposes is not of interest to you. But this new bank of ours will generally accept anything on our list, and if something is not on our list we'll be continually updating it to include it. We'll take virtually anything for credit purposes provided it can be stored without perishing, and we'll be looking into perishable items as well soon."

"How much do the card and the reader cost?"

"Nothin', Daisy! I can see yer interested in this and run an honest business. We're doing this as a promotion to get people like yer involved, and if yer interested in joining us, yer can act as our agent to distribute the cards to yer customers and the card plus reader combo to other traders."

"I don't rightly know what to say," she said finally. "See, we haven't seen stuff like this for years. Even if we had such things in stock, it'd sit there on the shelves. It's hand to mouth for most of me customers. Basic food's about all they can afford."

"We understand that," said Serge softly, "and to start with many of these things will either be free or paid for when yer customers can afford them. See we represent a foundation system which is also keen to help get people back on their feet. We need people like yer, who're willing to take our products and act as our agents. Eventually we're hoping to build a network of agents like yer."

"Sounds like yer'd be leaving me without a job without me livelihood. Do you realise what yer doing?" Daisy's mood had rapidly turned from wonderment to suspicion and fear.

"No, you'll be selling on commission at the list price for the item. Yer'll get yer commission immediately we're notified of the transaction. We'll stand 'bank' for yer until yer paid. And we won't hold it against yer if yer aren't. All we require from yer each month is a statement of receipts and outstanding debts against each item. That'll come to us automatically if yer using the special terminal we're providing yer with."

"I don't know about this. It all sounds a lot too complicated."

The two continued talking about the scheme for half an hour before Daisy finally made her mind up and agreed to become Prospect Bank's first local agent. Serge emerged from her shop beaming at the result of his morning's work. Daisy, not a person to be taken in, was also happy to go along with what this stranger had to offer her business.

« »

Sam had been happy to encourage Serge to run with this new idea. The 'Prospect Credit Bank', as they'd started calling it, had now been running for 6 months and had in many respects overshadowed Prospect's former role as a supplier of castings for the farm market. Serge wanted to explain progress with Sam over lunch and was able to show her a series of graphs generally positive after a slow take up.

Sam was looking relieved. "As you know I had my doubts about your idea right from the start. I could understand the logic of bank rather than barter, but my main concern was we were taking on too much and maybe becoming more visible than I'd have liked. There are increasingly the rival gangs who're starting to ignore the rule of law everywhere we go these days."

"That's it exactly. Prospect's never going to expand its markets, unless there's safer ways of exchange. And maybe it'll help fuel a wider bush-led recovery," said Serge.

Rodney Jensen

"Yes it's had my blessing and I'm glad it's going well."

"Well actually, there's more I need to tell yer," said Serge shifting the weight off his prosthetic foot.

"Oh?"

"See, Daisy who was my first serious customer, while firstly being quite suspicious-like, has become a big believer in the benefits. Her trade has grown so much she's had to build a storage area behind her store and open another place down the road."

"What's the problem with that?"

"No problem, except she's finding it difficult to keep up with all the paperwork, filling in the orders. But she's about to start deliveries soon and I can see she won't be able to cope. So I offered to become partner."

"And what would that entail?"

"Well several things. I'd like to move to 'er place— any other arrangement would not be practical, like. But ere's the part you and the others may not like. We want to borrow one or two andronics to help grow the business and maybe there'll be a need for more in the future."

"Wow. Have you mentioned this to Gem or Mayhew? I think they should be consulted about this."

"No I thought I'd run it past yer first."

"Personally I can't see a problem with the idea. It's no different from providing things for the guerrilla cells."

"In the first instance I think any andronic we use would need to be kept back-of-house. We don't want to lose all our customers from the start, that's fer sure."

"Well you should run with it as far as I'm concerned. I don't suppose that either of the others will mind, but please keep them in the loop. I guess my main issue is losing you." Sam was looking intently at Serge as she read his reaction, and threw in her next question casually. "Is this simply a business partnership or is there more to it?" Sam had never seen Serge blush before, but his awkward body language spoke volumes, almost making her laugh.

"Well er … that's something I ain't exactly checked with 'er first!"

"Probably time you did!" remarked Sam laughing. "Congratulations Serge!" Sam threw her arms around him in a bear hug that took him completely by surprise.

Just at this moment, Gem came into the room. He looked quizzically at Sam. "Serge's about to leave us, and I think he's in love!" said Sam laughing.

"Leave the man alone, can't you see how embarrassed yer making him," said Gem. Sam could see that Gem knew Serge well enough to have already guessed. It explained to her why Serge had seemed so damned cheerful of late— it hadn't been all about turning the rural economy around after all.

"Damn right!" was all that Serge could think of saying.

CHAPTER 25

Sam had mentioned to Mayhew: "We've been deploying an andronic here around the clock to check what's happening out there. Despite any assurances Leila may have given me, we want to be sure that the Aggressives have really given up their plans for global domination."

It piqued Mayhew's curiosity, and he began to take more of an interest in the communications room that Sam had helped establish. "None of our mobile cells are still active, are they?" he asked.

"No they're not. They stayed in place for several weeks after Alien City was abandoned, but it became impossible to insist they continue monitoring with nothing but silence day after day. This seems to confirm what I was told, but I have this nagging feeling the Aggressive are still around somewhere, which is why I have insisted on keeping this watch in place. It's an ideal duty for andronics, who don't really need to rest. But we still choose to switch them around, so that they're all familiar with what to look for."

"And that is?"

"Good question. I've theorised that if the Aggressives have moved their sphere of operation from Alien City to somewhere else on this planet, someone would have noticed, particularly if they had attempted to start their abductions again. I was hoping that in the absence of a reliable Holo-Net, some survivors out there might have resorted to short wave radio, which is technically not difficult for anyone to set up with basic components. There's stuff which could probably be scrounged. Oh, as you know, this is ADR-03 by the way," Sam introduced the andronic who was seated in front of something which excited keen interest by Mayhew.

"That's a communications transceiver," he breathed. "I haven't seen one of those since I was a boy. My uncle was a 'Ham', you see, he used to spend an inordinate amount of time chatting on the short wave bands with other Hams, until the internet took over in the '90s and interest in the hobby died completely. Where on earth did you find that?"

"We've been keeping it quiet, but while we were at Richmond, Gem and Serge tracked down a very old Ham operator. They noticed his large roof-mounted antenna. He gave us this set because he was getting too old to keep the system operational."

"It still works? It must be more than 70 years old!"

"Apparently yes, although I believe ADR-03 had to rectify one or two things?"

"My testing revealed two small components were malfunctioning," ADR-03 acknowledged. The transceiver is now fully operational after I replaced one of the circuit board capacitors and a burnt out resistor in the power supply."

"Have you received any messages? What are you listening to at the moment," Mayhew was beside himself and had momentarily regained the excitement of his youth. He could hardly resist wanting to put on a pair of headphones and to try softly rotating the large tuning knob.

ADR-03 expanded on his findings: "I can confirm I have monitored short wave radio activity on certain frequencies, but so far, we have not been able to build a comprehensive picture of where these operators are located, what their circumstances are, how often and on what frequencies we can expect to find them again."

"This is news to me. Why haven't I been told this before!" Sam exclaimed, resenting the fact she hadn't been informed and was caught unawares.

"This has really been my first opportunity to broach the subject, and we were waiting to advise you once a complete report was finalised," said ADR-03 unemotionally. "Many of the signals are coming from sources overseas, including the United States, Europe and Asia."

"Let's have a list please—we need to know firstly where any locals are sited and the places they are communicating with."

"That can be done of course, but it will first be necessary to improve both our short wave receiver and our antennas to enable greater direction finding capacity. We have discovered useful information on how to do this from the UFODD server, but it will take some time.

« »

It was several days before a team of three andronics had assembled a greatly improved transceiver and high gain directional antennas that could pinpoint the source of signals emanating from anywhere in the world. The first test proved anti-climactic, when ADR-03 reported to Sam, "the new equipment is providing far clearer signals now, but despite the technical improvements, we are still limited by the signal conditions. These vary greatly with the time of day and the state of the ionosphere. For the signals we have been able to monitor, it is also almost certain that we can return a message back to that source. However this would not be in accordance with the protocol you have laid down," said ADR-03 looking at Sam. She nodded her head in agreement.

Mayhew and Serge looked at Sam questioningly. "I thought the idea was to determine whether there are any further signs of alien activity?" queried Mayhew.

"Both you and ADR-03 are correct," said Sam. "The main thing we have to do is listen to what these operators are telling us. I am pretty sure if there is any alien activity occurring, that it will be reported. On the other hand, assuming for the moment it is still happening, it would be extremely inadvisable for us to telegraph our existence and new location."

"Have there been many messages?" Mayhew spoke directly to ADR-03.

"Yes many, but as yet we have not had sufficient time to build up a pattern."

"Evidence of alien activity?"

"No. None so far," he replied flatly.

"Okay, despite this, I must insist that for the time we maintain radio silence, just to be sure," said Sam. "If at some stage, because there is evidence of ongoing Aggressive activity, we may decide to interrogate the source, that would have to be done from another location rather than revealing this one."

Sam and the others agreed that ADR-03 and the other andronics should continue with the program of message interception, recording and tracking.

Rodney Jensen

Some days later, Sam was given a report on the signals that had been regularly monitored. It showed the call sign or nickname of the operator, the time it had been received, the frequency and the estimated location. She stared at a sample of the messages which had been recorded both verbatim and in translated form.

"They're from all over the place," she remarked. "This one sounds pretty terminal wouldn't you say?" She was pointing at a message from Northern Germany: *Helfen Sie uns, Wir sind dabei, von Banditen werden überrannt. Es wird nicht lange dauern, bis sie herausfinden, wo meine Station versteckt ist. (Help us, we're about to be overrun by bandits. It will not be long before they find out where my station is).*

"And this one at least sounds like he's got a sense of humour," she said: *On m'a terrée ici depuis trois ans maintenant et je vais prier pour la pluie (I've been holed up here for three years and I'm praying for rain).*

"I think this one's from Indonesian Borneo—might be more do-able for us if we were minded to rescue them: *Menunjuk rig di Sydney dan aku berharap seseorang di luar sana. (My rig's pointing at Sydney and I'm hoping someone's there.)*

But as Sam read a message from someone in one of the northern states of America she felt a tear welling up as it reminded her of Byron's origins and manner of speech. *Hey Guys! I'm done with listening to static and no one there. I know you're there but too cute to come out 'n play. I'm outa supplies here, it's getting real cold and it's move time—again! Call me, arrange a sked or sumpin'—it'd be good to hear another friendly voice if nuffin else. I've rigged up a solar panel which should keep this piece of shit goin' a while longer. Just means I have to broadcast during sunlight 'cause there ain't no batteries left! Pleeeeze call!*

There was nobody else there for Sam to talk to at that moment, but she had to discuss the messages with someone, and chose ADR-03 rather than bottling up her feelings. "What should we do? We are facing a humanitarian catastrophe. There must be thousands of people out there. We simply cannot rescue them all. But on the other hand there is no definite evidence of alien activity other than the German reference to 'bandits' which could literally mean that, or be code for aliens. Of all the messages we've received, I would like to check that one. What do you think?"

ADR-03 answered her without any pause. "Sam. You have already answered your own question. Assuming that you had the means to venture into any one of those places, the risk of interception would be enormous. At best you might on a single journey be able to bring back as many as ten individuals who would then be just as much at risk here in Australia as they already are."

"What about returning their signals then?"

"That can certainly be arranged, although I am unclear as to what purpose it would serve?"

ADR-03's remark was coldly logical but Sam tried to think of a reasoned response. "It might give them hope. If they were to form nodes of resistance, at some point in the future we will be able to supply them with weapons, weapons which they will be able to produce themselves if we were able to set up implementation capability like we have here," she said at last but not really even convincing herself that this could be possible.

"Yes I believe that idea has merit. But I would counsel you on being clear about your strategy before you embark on it. The risks are too high otherwise. Only once you have proved to yourself that the strategy is working should you attempt to involve other humans globally."

Sam said nothing but could not disagree. It simply was not the time to allow emotions to get the better of her. *They've made me their Commander in Chief and I've got to act like one!* she thought.

CHAPTER 26

Looking back, it was difficult for anyone to say precisely when the climate had met a point of no return, and weather conditions had taken on a new pattern. It didn't happen overnight, but the first obvious signs occurred in the 2051 winter, when there was an unusually heavy fall of snow over the Great Dividing Range (which separates coastal New South Wales from the continental inland). The snow not only covered the mountains for an abnormally long time, but spread far into the outback and lasted well into November, at a time when much hotter weather should have been starting.

By Christmas, there were still large patches of snow to be seen cladding the higher peaks and ridges. All the paddocks, their valleys and troughs in the landscape continued to be covered by heavy frost, particularly on south facing slopes, lasting well into the afternoon on a typical day. The summer months at the beginning of the new year finally experienced very high temperatures in mid-February, followed by a reversion to un-seasonally cold weather in March. The cold intensified across the whole country, until by August freezing temperatures were experienced again from former sub-tropical regions of Australia, right down as far as the southern coastline.

It was a weather pattern which did not change in subsequent years and people began to speak of the 'New Ice Age'. There was mounting fear that the trend was growing worse each season. Equally noticeable was the start of a drought that continued unabated in the interior. Areas of former subtropical rainforest gradually turned to dry wilderness. Extensive vegetation dieback had left formerly wooded tracts as sorry ranks of dead and dying trees and dry underbrush. There was no water left in the dams for sheep or cattle and crops failed, leaving the ground bare of vegetation and a source of ochre coloured dust whenever winds swept across now barren plains. For those who had escaped being rounded up by the FCs, the lack of reliable weather conditions suited to growing food, fuelled a continuing stream of land refugees walking off their properties never to return.

Life at Prospect was not so acutely affected as the places further to the west of the Dividing Range, but shortages of food and water were becoming an ongoing problem. Matters came to a head in the spring of 2053 when it became obvious that there was less than a month's reserve of drinking water and seemingly no prospect of rains to revitalise the market gardens.

Serge had been warning Sam about the situation for some time, and nothing had changed the day they met together with Mayhew and other key Prospect residents to discuss what to do. It was a freezing morning and all were clad in kangaroo skin bonnets, full length fur coats and leather ankle boots to ward off the cold in the draughty community shed where they were gathered. There was general agreement that the effects of the drought were so widespread that there seemed little to be gained by any suggestions of moving elsewhere. Serge had the floor and was breathing on his hands as he shuffled a few notes he was glancing at from time to time.

"I reckon we gotta assume there's not goin' to be any more big rains like we used to get 'ere. And there definitely ain't goin' to be water for irrigation any longer. But I'll bet yer there's still plenty of water underground. Jest got to find it's the problem. Anyone got any other ideas?"

"Don't forget where we are—on a hillside. Not the ideal place to find underground water is it?" suggested Sam.

"We won't know for sure 'til we try looking for it. I reckon we need a water diviner."

"And I suppose you have someone in mind?"

"As a matter of fact, I do. There's someone I heard of a while back who was recommended by a mate of mine in Gloucester. We could give 'im a try?"

George Hickson proved to be an elusive hayseed for Serge, who had travelled all the way to Gloucester to track him down. After the fifth place he'd last been seen, it became obvious he was much in demand when he wasn't propping up the bar in the nearest watering hole. Serge finally found him in a pub on the outskirts of Cessnock on a busy Friday evening. There was a roaring fire and the atmosphere was smoky and convivial as the combination of heat and booze lifted general morale against the freezing night time conditions outside.

Serge had been given a tip where to find him from one of the small farms nearby, and the publican pointed him out. He was sitting in a corner, regaling two or three other drinkers with stories of his successes and failures in finding water.

Rodney Jensen

Serge was well aware that despite there being no real explanation of *how water divining works*, most people in the bush respected the art, and could draw on cases where a successful bore had quite simply meant the difference between survival and disaster. George was no exception to the diviner's reputation, having a somewhat mystical aura about him with his stories. By the time Serge found him, he was already into his sixth beer, judging by the empties on the table next to him.

"Sure I'll take a look, but it'll have to wait a week or two—there's three places I've got to do round here first. Just give us a map or something and I'll come when I can," said the well lubricated George.

Serge had sketched out a map for him and had to be satisfied that George would live up to his promise. As it turned out, the casually suggested two weeks stretched into three and Serge was being pressured to find someone else, when the man turned up out of the blue at Prospect in a fifty year old Range Rover converted to a ute, and held together with fencing wire.

Serge greeted him warmly as he eased himself out of the cabin and looked appraisingly over the terrain, where the shacks and paddocks were located and where the production area was.

He produced his water divining wires—two lengths of fencing wire each bent at one end to form an L shaped handle, and started making soundings. He would hold each length of wire by the handles and point them forward as he walked along a chosen path. "They cross over each other when there's water below, there's something moves 'em none of us who've got the talent can explain it. But it works all right—time after time!" said George.

But after he had spent nearly two hours fruitlessly walking in various areas particularly where the contours might be associated with underground water lines, he drew a blank. "Most creeks got water under 'em," he said. "But unfortunately, there ain't no creeks which would collect water under them round here—too steep for that."

George wasn't going to give up easily and started looking further afield. It seemed he was enjoying hanging around the Prospect community. He turned out to know a lot more about farming than simply water divining and offered advice to those who were growing fruit and vegetables in their gardens, including the more winter-tolerant types and the need to establish hedges for shelter against the constant winds. But it was a chance encounter with Prospect's children which brought about an even greater reform than restoration of water supply.

The children had been fascinated to watch George at work and followed him around everywhere he went, trying to guess where he'd go next, hugely excited at the possibility of seeing the divining wires mysteriously crossing over each other. He was patient with them at first and even showed one or two of them how to hold the wires. But after a frustrating day of finding no promising leads, finally lost his cool, threw his wires to the ground and strode over to Sam who'd been watching him at a discreet distance. "Haven't them bloomin' kids got sumpin' better to do?" he demanded. "How come they ain't got lessons or things to do around their 'omes. The little buggers is spoilin' me concentration."

Sam tactfully told the children to leave George alone as he needed to be left in peace. She was reluctant to admit to George that nothing had been done about setting up a school, but his caustic remark set her thinking and she decided it was high time to take action.

« »

Sam turned firstly to their andronics to work out how to provide basic courses in practical subjects that would contribute to the daily lives of the community. Then she thought it was time to discuss her concerns with the others, but was pleasantly surprised to discover that both Serge and Mayhew liked the idea from slightly different angles.

"The only future for these kids lies in education," she'd said to Serge and Mayhew at another special meeting. "We're living in a world of huge transitions and our children need to be equipped to understand and work with the changes."

"Been thro' it meself remember—or rather the lack of any schoolin'. So don' expect me to disagree with yer! Question is what yer goin to do about it?"

Mayhew, educator all his life, proved a more practical contributor than the others might have expected, and would have gladly taken on full responsibility but for his failing health, deteriorating eyesight and poor hearing, all pretty normal for a man in his late 70s. "That sounds like a good start," he said. "Given our situation I think we must emphasise basic survival skills as might have been learned by our indigenous people. Things like hunting, gathering, cooking and shelter and understanding plants not only for eating but medicinal purposes."

"Well I've got to hand it to yer. I had yer pegged as dyed-in-the-wool thinker not doer! But what you come up with is what they need for sure!" said Serge. "Got to start with the simple stuff, like readin for example. Readin's important of course, but next they want to learn is how to defend themselves in a fight and patch themselves up if they get hurt."

Don't forget we're dealing with children and not adults!" Sam said. She turned to ADR-03, who had proved so helpful in the communications room. "Have you got any other suggestions?"

"I have been listening to this discussion with great interest because it highlights for me how different humans are from beings who practise logic-based thinking, the type which we andronics use. If children are trained to use advisers like me, or understand how to access information sources easily, they no longer need the traditional 'reading writing and arithmetic' concerns of your cultural past."

"But what about practical skills? That's things they've got to be taught and you can't really read it out of a book or get from an android can yer?" said Serge.

"OK! We hear you and will take your important practical concerns on board, Serge. This discussion has been a big help thanks, but I am going to work something out now and ADR-03 will help me implement the pilot program for Prospect. We'll see how that goes and review progress in six months.

You'll get your opportunities then to tell us where we've gone wrong! Meeting's over," said Sam.

Eventually, George had to travel 3 km down the slope below Prospect to a creek bed before finding any worthwhile underground water. After weeks of carting water to and from the new source to Prospect, Serge organised a new narrow diameter pipeline. Its purpose was to carry pumped water from the bore to a header tank in the village. On the day that the system was brought on stream, widespread relief was felt among all the village dwellers. Once again, they would have a fresh supply of water for drinking, washing and watering their market gardens. But George sounded a cautionary note: "Don't expect there'll be water 'ere forever. If we don't get some rain the chances are this akifer's goin' to dry up. So don't waste it and then come runnin' to me complainin'. I done the best I can. It's what I always say to me customers. I can't work miracles yer know!"

CHAPTER 27

By 2054 life in Prospect and surrounding areas had settled into a new sense of peace and normality. One late afternoon Sam stood on the school room veranda watching with a feeling of satisfaction, children emerging from their classroom. She was reflecting on what she Mayhew and ADR-03 had accomplished. The children were of mixed ages, equally varied in their learning abilities and unused to the confines of the new classroom. Of necessity, lessons were interactive and practical, and were held as much outside, as inside the school. Many of their parents confessed to Sam they felt that they were benefitting from the new teaching and training as much as their children.

As the exuberant group scampered past her, chattering and excited to be free for the day, she was feeling that she had achieved something more positive and relevant to Prospect's future than anything else she could have done, *apart from challenging the threat of the Aggressives, establishing a more reliable water supply and a stable trading economy*, she reminded herself.

She looked up and saw a figure, the sun behind him, approaching in her direction. It was hard to make him out in silhouette, but as she stared more intently, his walk and shape made the hairs on her neck tingle. "Hiram, it's you. What are you doing here? Serge told me a long time ago that you'd gone away and probably wouldn't be back?"

"You're the reason I changed my mind Sam. You're looking great," he continued awkwardly.

Rodney Jensen

"Let's go up to the village and I'll introduce you to some people you haven't met. We've still got Gem and Mayhew here, but Serge has moved in with a woman called Daisy ..."

"Yes I remember that, she was mentioned in despatches. Serge has been in touch with me from time to time. I know how you feel so I haven't ..."

"Hiram it's been a long time. When Serge told me that you were going away for good, I put aside any long term plans or feelings that I might have held onto for us. I've been busy here and I feel a sense of achievement in what we're doing. Please don't dredge up the past and make me unhappy all over again will you?"

"Sam, I know I haven't been fair to you. But I had ghosts to deal with; I couldn't start anew without at least trying to discover what happened to my family."

"And now you've worked that out—what should've been obvious from the start, you're coming here and expecting me to be available. It's the first time you have ever made the journey to Prospect. How do you think that makes me feel?"

"You've a right to be angry. If you want me to go I'll go. But let me just explain a little more why I've been away so long."

"Let's go and have something to eat, you can tell me then.

Rogers was a good story teller, and despite her anger, Sam could not resist wanting to learn more about his adventures.

"I realised that I had to travel back States-side to find out what happened to my folks—mom and pop, my wife Tina, my son Dave and daughter Katie. There was never any word from them after the pandemic, but that didn't necessarily mean they had all been infected. It could simply have been the fact that there was no way they could contact me or find out where I was. Even though in my heart of hearts I saw little chance of finding any of them alive, I felt I must try to learn what had happened before I could commit fully to our relationship."

Sam could easily have told Rogers to "go take a hike!" at this point, but resisted the urge and held her tongue.

"The first problem was to find a way of travelling that far. I thought of all the options such as building a sailing boat, hitching a ride with someone who already had a yacht or maybe if I could find my way up to Queensland, see if there was anyone still looking for deck hands on some cargo ship or other. In the end I decided the best and quickest thing was to re-visit the drone design we have, get rid of its bomb bays and substitute passenger space for me and enough storage for food and other supplies for a week at least. I calculated it could make the journey from Sydney to San Francisco in less than 48 hours."

"You mean you flew from Sydney to San Francisco by yourself on a drone?" Sam breathed quietly in amazement.

"That's right, entirely on solar power. I just set the auto-pilot, sat back and we got there. Though finding a landing spot was not so straightforward and I crashed the drone trying to land on what turned out to be a field covered in ditches and rubbish. I was lucky to come out alive, even before I really started my search. Anyway I got out with just a few cuts and bruises and began walking to my first destination. I had landed on the campus of what used to be Menlo College, which is located close to where the family home was in Silicon Valley. The streets there had a lot of fancy houses on large pieces of land, but they're all in ruins and the family home's no exception. The streets used to be lined with large leafy trees but they've all been chopped down for firewood. When I arrived at my house, I was bailed up by a pretty unfriendly character with an automatic at the ready, so I high-tailed it out of there without bothering to argue the toss."

"Not a great start!" remarked Sam.

"No, it was obvious if my family had survived the pandemic, they were long gone from our family home. I pondered whether they might have left word with someone and remembered the local pastor who we were friendly with. He officiated when we were married, and he seemed impressed by my DELTEX credentials. So, I found my way to the chapel we worshipped in, which was as empty and desecrated as you might expect."

"Then I had my first break. I found someone working in the graveyard, an old lady I didn't at first recognise, but for some reason she recognised me. It was my primary school teacher, and she spotted me first. We'd invited her to our wedding because I always felt I owed her such a lot for tolerating even encouraging my obsession with electronics. She was an enlightened woman, Hilda Braidmoor, and there she was, pulling weeds from the graves, unrecognisable with her hair tied back in a scarf and wearing a dirty pinafore and boots and looking so much older than the young woman I remembered."

"Did she know anything about your family?"

"She did, that's the amazing thing. But it was more than difficult for her to tell me about it. Maybe it was because of the wedding that she kept an interest in our family and knew exactly what happened. My mom and pop were the first to go she said, they'd moved in with my wife and children because they thought Silicon Valley would be safer than where they were living, holed up in an apartment in central San Fran. But they became infected almost immediately, and unintentionally took my wife and son with them. Hilda finally showed me where they were buried. She dug the grave herself for the four of them. It's unmarked." Rogers paused to wipe a tear. Sam felt real sympathy for his profound grief and tried to be patient, as she waited to hear the part of the story she guessed he was coming to.

"You're probably wondering what happened to Katie?" he said at last, once he'd reined in his emotions. "Well here's the thing. Katie's alive and well, married and has a family of her own. It turns out that beside Katie and her husband, I have a grandson and two grand-daughters living in California. Hilda took me to meet them all. They're happy, but of course it was a bitter sweet re-union. Katie was 12 at the time she lost her grandparents, mother and brother. She thought I was dead too, and if it hadn't been for Hilda, would definitely not have survived herself. Hilda took her in for the next few years and they helped each other."

"So I found myself effectively a stranger to them all. It left me a dilemma. I could offer them a new but uncertain life in Australia. But how could I be responsible for so many other lives, united by family feelings alone. In any case, none of them wanted to come with me to Australia. It was too much of a leap for them. They had managed to find a reasonably secure place to live, and they weren't about to give that up having survived the maelstrom.

"So I felt I had to come back here, Sam for you whom I love deeply. My feelings are the same, I think we've remained emotionally attached, even if that's not how you feel. Now that I know how things stand in America, I'm no longer tethered by uncertainty. There's no reason, except time and neglect on my part for us to be together. That is of course unless you have found someone else?" Sam merely shook her head, her face stony.

"Listen Sam, I just came here hoping that you might find it in your heart to forgive me. From your point of view I can understand you might not be able to do that. If you agree, I'll stay here a day or two, however long it takes for you to come to terms with this new situation. I'm ready to offer you everything I have, do whatever you want me to do. You probably don't even know yourself which way to turn right now, that's OK as far as I'm concerned. If you want me to go, I'll go and I'll understand but I hope you give me a chance which I know I don't really deserve."

Sam drew a breath and stared at the school room for a full minute before coming to a decision. "OK," she responded without any softening or commitment in her tone. "We'll find you a nice quiet place for you to stay in for the time—even give you some work so you can earn your keep—but there are no guarantees about us, not the way I'm feeling at the moment."

"That's understood. I'm sorry to have caused you such a shock. I couldn't think of any easier way."

"OK then. I'll ask ADR-03 here to look after your needs, meanwhile I must tell the others the good news."

With that Sam walked away purposefully, leaving Rogers to stare after her with a far-away look in his eyes.

It was two weeks later, when Sam's feelings for Rogers were finally resolved for her. She decided that she felt rage rather than gratitude at being re-connected. She'd done her soul-searching years before, and an essential part of the process had been learning to let him go. And here he was again. *Can it be possible for me to pick up where we've left off when I've let him go and even stopped thinking about him for so long?* That was the question which continually haunted her and for which she could find no ready answer.

Matters came to a head when Rogers finally made the decision to leave. That morning she discovered the shack where he'd been bunking down was deserted. He'd left a brief note for her on the table which read:

Honey, it's taken a while for me to accept that things are not going to be the same between us, and my presence here is causing you a lot of grief. So I'm heading off. One possibility

Rodney Jensen

is to return to America although common sense tells me I'm not really needed there either and my future lies in this country. I guess I'll make a new life somewhere. I can't leave you a forwarding address because I've no idea where I'll be. Take care and be happy. My fondest love Hiram.

Sam's reaction surprised only those who didn't really understand her. She felt a wash of sorrow and anger, screaming for Gem to come and help find him. "He doesn't know this area. He's unarmed as far as I know. I don't want to have his getting himself killed on my conscience!"

Serge also came up to Prospect to help in the search. He understood probably better than her what her feelings were. He organised two of their ADRs to check all the nearby tracks and roads in MAGs, and Sam went with one of them. Serge also mobilised one of their drones to make some aerial passes within a 50 km radius of Prospect.

It was three days before Sam and her ADR-03 driver finally found Rogers, helping George Hickson with his water divining services on a property not far from Gloucester. The land and aerial searches had proved fruitless and the search party had resorted to checking hotels in the region. As the publican of the 'Gloucester Arms' recalled: "This Yank feller turned up one evening. Looked like he'd been sleeping rough and fell in with George Hickson, one of our regulars here. They had a few drinks—the man reckoned he could do with a few bucks, and I overheard George offering 'im work to help him on something he'd lined up around here. As far as I know the gent accepted the offer because they left the bar together."

"Do you by any chance happen to know where this property is?" asked Sam.

"Well as a matter of fact I do. Belongs to me cousin, Bill Thurston. 'im and 'is Missus been there for years. They've run out of water like most places round here. I put 'em onto George because I know how well respected 'e is at divining like …"

"Can you show us how to reach this property?" Sam interrupted.

The publican drew her a mud-map on one his beer coasters. "Snot far—yer can't miss it," he promised.

By this time it was getting late and she decided to wait until morning to resume the search. She spent a troubled night, unable to relax or sleep instead lying awake, tossing and turning, questioning her own sanity. In her conflicted state of mind she could not begin to understand why she was so gutted by Rogers' sudden departure from Prospect AND before they'd had a chance to really talk things through properly. *Was it a sense of guilt? Was it really fear for his safety—a grown, experienced man, totally capable of looking after himself? She had to admit that she had powerful feelings for him after all. Her resistance was merely a defence mechanism. She simply didn't want to get hurt again.* She sat up in bed as this realisation hit her. She scrambled out of bed, dressed quickly and set off without any further delay giving directions to the farm to ADR-03 in the pre-dawn light.

The mud map proved to be a very poor guide, and she was forced to call into two other properties along the way before she finally found a farm gate with the 'Thurston' sign nailed to it, some 30 km from Gloucester. The farm was located in flat country, and from the gate she almost immediately spotted two figures in the distance, one of whom she immediately recognised.

"Hiram!" she shouted, having piloted the MAG to the closest point she could get along the entrance track, scrambled over a barbed wire fence and began to run the final two hundred metres across a grassy paddock. The two men stopped what they were doing and Rogers started walking towards her, finally breaking into a run himself. The two almost collided mid-field.

"Honey, what are you doing here!"

"You bastard!" she cried and threw her arms around him in a passionate embrace.

George watched on at discreet distance, unsure what was going to happen next, but they finally they broke apart and walked over to him. "Thank you for looking after Hiram," she said to him, wiping her eyes, "but he could definitely do with a wash!"

"If you can help us find some water, on this 'ere property, then we might be able to oblige yer," said George with a chuckle.

THE END

Please review this novel

I hope that you enjoyed 'Covert Citadel'. I would appreciate it if you could spare a few moments to write a sentence or two in review. This helps other readers to decide if it is something they might also enjoy, and also it very much helps me as an author.

If you like, put a review where you purchased the book or on Amazon.

Alternatively go to my webpage:

www.rodneyjensenbooks.com

There is a review link on the Covert Citadel Book Page

《　》

Acknowledgments

This final edition has benefitted from the primary help of Liz McCarthy, my partner, editor, website designer and publisher. The gestation of this novel has taken longer than anything else I have written, originally commenced in 2015. Much of the original writing was encouraged by my late wife Joanne Winstanley, 1953-2018. Similarly a close friend, the late Jenny Towndrow Wilson, a former London based publisher, provided much forensic help and encouragement. For some time, the manuscript lay dormant before going through several further updates.

Pem Gerner, a former co-editor of the newsletter 'Cityscape' which we published 2005-2015, has provided invaluable advice, as has Philip Joy a long term friend and lover of literature. Another fount of invaluable help has been provided by members of the Northern Beaches Writers' Group, headed by Zena Shapter, and its members including Guy Hallowes, 'Füzzy' Mijmark and Tony McFadden.

《 》

About the author

Rodney Jensen is a speculative fiction writer focused on how current trends will shape the near future. Many of his ideas have been influenced by recent global pandemic events and his interests in artificial intelligence, the search for extra-terrestrial intelligence (SETI), and the recent estimation of a myriad exoplanets in our own galaxy, and beyond, based on recent astronomical evidence. The notion of cosmic-scaled artificial intelligence networks waiting for the appropriate time to make first contact with humankind is a pivotal turning point both in this novel and the prequel 'Covert Messages'.

Rodney Jensen

Reviewers' comments on Rodney Jensen's books

Covert Messages - *"If you enjoy futuristic science fiction and extra-terrestrial experiences, this is the book for you. The references to the past COVID-19 pandemic are chilling and force you to consider our own current situation, as the more serious pandemic of 2035 unfolds in the book. Rodney Jensen utilises his knowledge of Australian geography as he weaves a sombre tale, but includes the more positive romance or two as well."* **Elizabeth Saadeh**

« »

Tales for the Time Traveller - *"…a number of common themes emerge, which tie the collection together nicely. The role of technology, especially ongoing debates regarding its exploitation, and the rise of AI, feature prominently. A sense of exploration is also at the heart of the collection, both in terms of physical space (deserted island, new planets, outer space) and big ideas (such as tradition vs. progress, and what is 'real' vs. what is 'fake'—and how can we tell the difference, anyway?)"* **Chloe Barber-Hancock**

« »

Covert State - *"The novel is a well-paced traditional detective story set in the near future with a concealed sci-fi twist. The characters are engaging, skilfully presented as people you may already know. It takes you on a journey through Adelaide and its Hills, Sydney and the enigma that is Indonesia and its stormy relationship with Australia. An easy to read and most enjoyable Australian crime novel."* **Andy McGee**

« »

Other books by Rodney Jensen

www.ingramcontent.com/pod-product-compliance
Lightning Source LLC
Chambersburg PA
CBHW022015120726
47902CB00012B/273